THE GODS' SCION:

CHILD OF TEMPUS

BOOK ONE

WINNIFRED TATAW

ISBN-13: 978-1-79-444663-2

DEDICATION

This book is dedicated to my family and all those who helped make my dream a reality.

TABLE OF CONTENTS

HELLO READER...

Before you begin the journey of reading this book, take time to read the three "Stories of Earth." Think of these as reference guides for the lore of the book. I hope you enjoy it.

THE GODS

There was nothing until the big bang and the birth of Hapesire, the God of Space. Once space was born, Tempus, the God of Time, followed. With the creation of time came the creation of Vitae, the God of Life. Lastly, with life came Mors, the God of Death. They are the founding Gods of all things, the Deorumars (Dee–or–mars). Most refer to them as The Gods.

Hapesire gave us our dimensions, universes, planets, cosmos, zodiacs, black holes, space portals, and stars. Tempus gave us the seasons or Condoras (Con–door–as), the Epochs (days, weeks, months, and years), the Allos (slumber, memories, fate, and prophecy) past, future, and present. Vitae gave us Sentinels (living spirits and guardian angels), the Seven Essentials of Life (air, water, shelter, food, culture, productivity, and socialization), emotion, the Seven Virtues (chastity, charity, temperance, diligence, forgiveness, kindness, and humility), new, hope, miracles, and faith. Mors gave us Vigors (corrupted or ennui spirits), the Seven Deadly Sins (lust, envy, wrath, gluttony, pride, sloth, and greed), the underworlds, grief, and ghosts.

It may seem like a lot, but there is a child or demigod who rules over that factor in each section. For Space, they are called Satellites. For Time, they are called Apostles. For Life, they are called Votaries. For Death, they are called Sycophants.

All four Gods live in their dimensions: Taporis for Time, Spatium for Space, Himlen for Life, and Baratrus for Death. Though Hapesire's dimension is in space, it is invisible and intangible. Vitae's realm is only reachable by the children of the Gods and Acolytes (the Gods' bridge between their dimension and Earth). Tempus' dimension is only attainable by the Acolytes. Only in Mors' realm may other living beings enter, though they will lose their spirit and die if they stay too long.

Many worships these Gods. A single race may devote themselves to one or two Gods in particular. Over time many religions or cult followings have developed, even though only a few people have seen the Gods, usually through dreams or visions. They do not visit people. Instead, they enjoy watching from behind the scenes.

The Gods see each other as equals; however, they are not equal in power. Even the Gods have distinct personalities.

Time is patient, calm, collected, playful, and wise.

Space is lazy, stubborn, easy-going, and imaginative.

Life is curious, loving, giving, kind, understanding, and vibrant.

Death is discreet, calm, watchful, and unpredictable.

Now that you know the story of the Gods, may they watch over you as you continue reading this story.

THE ACOLYTES

The Gods saw a disconnection between themselves and the beings of Life—all living things on all planets, particularly Earth (the first planet created with life). They made the Acolytes serve as a bridge between Earth, the dimensions of the Gods, and the Gods themselves.

Each incarnated uniquely, depending on God. All are born on Earth. There are only ever four in existence. Each Acolyte has been blessed with its own set of powers and abilities. They are usually the beings closest to the Gods. The race of these Acolytes ranges across the board. An Acolyte of Death is chosen at birth. They will have the Emblem mark of Mors on their arm and be the opposite sex of the last Acolyte. They are always Umbrian, pure white, with vibrant eyes and jet-black hair. The female is called Lady Death, while the male is called Grim Reaper. They function as their namesake says, dealing with dead spirits. Their purpose on Earth is to guide souls to Baratrus, as well as to cleanse Vigors. They cannot kill. They only can take the spirits of those that are already dead.

They have a 'curse' upon them. A living being cannot touch them with their bare hands them. If they do, that living being's spirit is disembodied into a part of the Baratrus. Their spirit can be recovered, but it can take months or years to find it. To place the soul back into the body is almost impossible. No one, not even the Acolyte of Death, knows why the 'curse' is the way it is. No one dares to ask Mors for an explanation.

The Acolyte of Life is the same as the Acolyte of Death with its rules of incarnations, though they can be any race and gender. Their purpose different is different on Earth as well. Acolytes of Life bless newborns with life (think of it as a well-wishing for long and happy life). They guide Mir (the Votary of Miracles), Faith (the Votary of Faith), Hope (the Votary of expectation and desire for good happenings), and New (the Votary of birth, growth, and renewal) to their destinations of need. These four Votaries are the only beings born from the Gods that regularly dwell on Earth. Gifted with feathered wings and golden hair, the Acolyte of Life also prevents unruly deaths such as suicides and murders for all living things. Along with the Acolyte of Death, the Acolyte of Life is the most active on Earth.

The last two Acolytes' purpose and jobs on Earth get a little more confusing and complicated.

The Space Acolyte works directly with Milky (the daughter of Hapesire and the embodiment of galaxies, cosmos, and space portals). The Space Acolyte works as a planner for Milky. They travel together between universes through space portals they open, fixing problems in the places they visit. The creation of a new Space Acolyte is chosen both by Milky and the current Space Acolyte. The child becomes an Acolyte officially between the age of five to ten. The child is reborn with mixed blue and purple hair with light-colored eyes. Once they are chosen, Milky comes to Earth and takes the child with her, raising them as her own. She is one of the few children and demigods to have such a caring, close and guiding relationship with an Acolyte of the Gods.

Lastly, we come to the Acolyte of Time. They are the most offhand of the Acolytes. They are also the Acolytes that go through minor physical changes upon their rebirth. The only difference being the addition of the Tempus Emblem to their forearm. They are born after the earlier Acolyte has died. Their primary purpose is to prevent others from disrupting the time-space continuum. As the statement before suggests, they also often go with the Space Acolyte. Their other tasks include regulating the Seasons on Earth, monthly checks on the amount of sleep dust being distributed and communicating the events of Earth directly to Tempus. This is especially important during times of war, famine, drought, etc.

THE PEOPLE OF EARTH

On Earth, there are 8 billion people. With a wide variety of races existing on Earth, from humans to mermaids, life on the planet is colorful and exotic. There are four categories of the races on Earth: Water Marrows, Earth Marrows, Air Marrows, and Fire Marrows.

People that fall into the Water Marrow category are Mermaids, Jengus, and Sirens. All Water Marrows can manipulate water. They can only do this with oceanic water and freshwater sources (lakes, rivers, streams, etc.). All people in this race have gills. Mermaids have human-like torsos and faces, with the lower halves of their bodies made up of colorful fishtails, resembling those of Bettas or Angelfish. Jengus are like Mermaids, but they are darker in skin tone, have green hair and orange tails. Unlike the Mermaids, Jengus can morph their tail fins into fish-scaled legs.

Lastly are the Sirens. They are the only Water Marrows that do not have fishtails. They all have scales, some in patches, some head to toe. They can survive on land the longest—compared to the other Water Marrows (Jengus –ten hours, Mermaids – two and a half hours, and Sirens twenty-eight hours).

Earth Marrows, by far, have the most categories of people in their class. They include Humans, Umbrians, Cyborgs, and Illusionists. Humans are the largest group of Earth Marrows and people. They have no special abilities; except they have the most flexible DNA out of all races. That means that if they partner with any other species, 99% of the time, the child has many of the same traits as the parent who is not Human.

Umbrians come in second as the most prominent Earth Marrow subgroup on Earth. They are known for their skin enriched with melanin, vibrant eye colors (blues, greens, and golds), thick and natural hair patterns, and shadow abilities. Umbrians have control over Sanikins (pronounced: Sss-ann-ee-k-inn) or shadow puppets. They can create and manipulate the shadows of anything through making Sanikins, but they must come from a source near them. They can also phase through solid objects.

Cyborgs are a mixed group. Any group of people's races can be classified within this race. If at least 45.5% of their body is made up of robotic, metal, or cybernetic parts, they are classified as Cyborg. So, an Umbrian with 50% of their body robotic; are an Umbrian Cyborg. Human Cyborgs, however, are simply called Cyborgs.

Finally, there are the Illusionists. They are human-like but have magical powers and abilities. Their powers only work on living beings of Vitae and consist of spells, curses, charms, enchantments, etc. They can move non-living things in various ways but cannot change the physical or inner workings. Illusionists' magic and spells only last for short periods but are immensely powerful. The more power multiple Illusionists put into a spell, the longer it will last. Their magic is generated by two things: the number of spirits and Vigors in the area they are in and their surroundings. Most of their charms and enchantments come from vegetation, which are grown naturally from the Earth, which explains why their magic is so weak on technology.

Fire Marrows consists of Serpents and Drakonians. Serpents are like Mermaids and Sirens, but they have human-like torsos and faces with the lower halves of their bodies as snake forms. Or they could be covered head to toe in snake scales or patches, for them. They mostly live-in scorching areas, usually underground. They have heightened senses of sight and smell, as well as venom sacs in their fangs and nails. Their venom is twice as dangerous as Drakonians.' However, it takes more time to affect the victim. go into effect.

Due to their various abilities, Drakonians are considered one of the most powerful races on Earth. They can protract wings from their backs; they have retractable layers of scales in their skin, can produce flames from their bodies, have incredible vision during the day and night, can hear exceptionally well (mostly this is a trait of males), have retractable fangs and claws and can have nullifying or burning venom in their fangs or claws (this is most prominent in females). Most Drakonians do not retract their scale exteriors because they are used for protection and are hard to support. Even without the scaled skin, their 'cover' skin has a rough feel. They usually have warm-colored hair (reds, yellows and oranges) and deep-colored eyes.

Last of all are Air Marrows. They consist of Harpies, Fairies, and Pixies. Fairies and Pixies are miniature Humans that have wings. Fairies are larger. The tallest Fairy can reach up to four and a half feet, while the tallest Pixie can be one foot, two inches in height. Both can sense spirits, Illusionists, and Vigors. They possess environmental magic. This means that depending on which area they inhabit, the magic they use adapts to it. Their magic consists of changing the chemical makeup of one thing to another. For those living in forests, they could turn fire into tree branches (if they are living in a forest). They usually live in wooded areas or vast plains. Fairy wings resemble that of butterflies, while Pixies' wings resemble dragonflies.

Harpies are the most distinguished category race on Earth. They can have a mix of Human and bird body parts. Their bird parts resemble those of birds of prey. More than half of their population has winged appendages and beaks. The wings can be arm appendages or back appendages. All Harpies have large eyes, feathers, and ear-piercing cries.

NOW THAT YOU HAVE READ THE STORIES OF EARTH, IT IS TIME TO BEGIN YOUR JOURNEY THROUGH THE REST OF THE BOOK.

ENJOY.

CHAPTER ONE

His Illusory Realm

My eyes shot open. I was lying alone on the ground. My forearm was glowing; the Emblem of Tempus was the culprit.

I stood up and saw a narrow path in front of me, and a light appeared at the end. I start to walk.

As I continued down the mysterious path, a light appeared at the end of the trail.

Finally, I got to the end of the trail.

There are two ancient doors in front of me. I pushed them open, eager to know what was on the other side. The doors swung open, and the light reappeared. I reached out, barely grazing my fingers on it when I was transported to another place. I looked down at my arm, and a large flash of light shines over my eyes.

A giant temple was now in front of me, drenched in gold and ivory with its pillars looming, standing firm and tall. I walked up the stairs of the glorious temple to the two large doors at the front. I reach to pull the door open.

In the blink of an eye, I was back on the trail. I peered around to see where the door and the temple had gone. When I twisted around, I found it. Now there was a staircase leading up to it. The Emblem is on a pedestal at the very top. The sun and the moon glow like beacons in the darkness. The center circle pulled like waves of golden light.

As I got closer to the stairway, my arm blazed brighter. I heard others making indiscernible noises, but as I got closer, I noticed that it was repetitive,

"He will rise."

"He will rise."

"He will rise."

"He will rise."

The path behind me shakes and crumbles. I need to get closer.

The voices grew louder. The light from my arm became blinding. The chant begins to speed up as I get closer to the Emblem.

"He will rise. He will rise. He will rise. He will rise."

My anxiety grew with each moment, and I started to run faster, praying the path behind me did not pull me into the unknown black abyss.

I could feel the sweat on my body start to form. I heard my heart pounding in my chest. I will never reach the stairs.

"He will rise. He will rise. He will rise. He will rise."

The voices grow louder and louder.

My legs hurt. My palms are sweaty. My head was spinning.

"He will rise! He will rise! HE WILL RISE! HE WILL RISE!"

I was almost there; I could feel it.

If I could only get closer—

"PRINCE RODRICK!"

I jumped up, realizing it was a dream.

Man, I swear that felt all too real—

"My prince, a moment of your precious time."

Crap.

I was in Dr. Rosary's World Government Class. It was the end of my morning classes, thank goodness.

I heard some students laughing and snickering on their way out of the classroom.

"Any day now, Mr. Rodrick. I would like to get out of here sometime today."

I rolled my eyes and got up. What happened to the "Prince" part of my name?

He scowled as I made my way down the rows of chairs over to the fat, older man's desk.

"What did I *not* do now?" I asked him.

"Mr. Rodrick, what you are *not* going to do is pass my class by sleeping. I don't care who your mother is or who you are either. I went over some important—"

I blocked him out.

I was used to the whole "failing my class" speech. I will pass it anyway; I always did. Like he had the guts to fail a prince of the country he lived in.

"Are you even listening to me?"

I focused my eyes on the balding man. "No."

His bushy brows furrowed even more. He leaned back in the chair. "It's a shame, you may run this country one day, and you cannot even stay awake for a sixty-minute class."

"I have three other siblings, so don't try that crap with me. I'll pass your class; Queen Riva pays your check, and we don't need to talk anymore."

Before he could snap back, I got the rest of my things from the class and made my way out the door.

Parked outside, waiting for me, were four Royal Guard vehicles.

I groaned. I hated the Royal Guard; I could take care of myself better than those paid idiots. The second car's back seat passenger window rolled down, and Mrs. Erma's face appeared.

"You're late."

"I know, sorry," I smiled as the old lady rolled her eyes, opening the door for me. "You know the Annual Jovial Meeting is today, right?"

I knew, but I did not care. "I'm not planning on going."

She let out a breath. "That will simply be adding to the fire since the Queen is mad at you."

"Isn't she always mad at me?"

She turned to me, but I ignored her. I already knew what was coming when I got to the Castle. It was the same thing day in and day out.

"What did I do now?"

"She did not say." Mrs. Erma said, her eyes never meeting mine. "She did not seem to be in the best of moods when it came time to pick you up."

"Is she sober?"

Her jaw tightened. "For the time being, yes."

We made it back to the Castle in silence. Mrs. Erma told me Riva wanted me to go straight to her office. Walking down the Castle halls, I passed by busy staff members, various paintings, and vases.

When I reached her office door, I opened it; what.

I found was Riva working on a pile of papers. Next to them was a picture of me and my three siblings, Rayden, Rahima, and Rona.

An unopened bottle of wine sat lonely on the far corner of her desk. So, she was sober, for now, of course.

"You are late," she greeted me without looking up.

"I am always late," I said.

"Another failing grade?" she glanced at me.

"I'll pass the final exam. It's not important. It's a World Government Class. I don't need to pay attention to it. Plus, if I don't pass on my own, you'll make sure I do. So why am I—"

"It is not merely your World Government Class, is it?"

The room went quiet.

"I keep getting calls from the university."

"Don't answer them," I said.

They aren't supposed to be calling her anyway. I am the student, not her.

She paused and exhaled.

"If you would pass your classes, I wouldn't have to worry about them calling me."

I sucked my teeth. "Is this all you want to say to me?"

She scowled. "Your clothes for tonight are already set out up in your room. I want you to behave and function as if you have some decency when we get to—"

"Who told you I'm going anywhere?" I asked.

Since I was nine, she knew that I had not gone to a single Jovial Meeting or any events like it. I did not like those people, and they did not like me.

She put down her pen. "Close the door."

I eyed her curiously and did as I was told.

"Rodrick, this meeting with the other nations will not only be on better international borders, poverty intervention, and refugee inflation. We are adding another topic to this year's list of problems."

I gave her a dirty look. "Such as?"

She breathed out. "Ryton."

My head perked up, and she continued.

"Due to the increase in terrorist and rebellion uprisings, I strongly believe the Atar is reforming and growing larger than it was decades ago."

I stepped closer to her desk. "You guys are going to sit around for three hours straight to talk about a guy that died sixteen years ago and his terrorist group? That's wonderful. What does that have to do with me?"

She scowled at me. "You know as well as I do that, he is not dead."

I scoffed. "If he were, I wouldn't have had to go through all this crap with you—"

She raised her hand to stop me from continuing. "Rodrick. Do not start. I did not ask you to come here and cry about things in the past that I cannot change."

She lowered her hand. "We will also be discussing you and how you can be ready—"

I stopped her there. "To be used as a weapon, or 'key,' or whatever you want to call me? Riva, I am not going to go so I can have people decide on how I best benefit their needs."

Not a word came out of her lips.

I twisted around, aiming to leave her office. I paused, turning back around. "Why did you even tell me this? I will not be in the room while you and your 'friends' talk."

Her dark blue eyes stared at me, impassive. "I wanted to inform you because most likely, we will be calling you into the room. You will have a voice in deciding how you can help us take on this situation."

After everything you put me through...well, I guess it would lead up to this.

I headed out the door.

"The plane leaves at 4:45," she yelled after me.

"I won't be there, Riva," I exclaimed as I slammed the door shut.

In my room, I noticed the suit on my bed.

It was composed of a fitted, narrow-notch navy blue coat, black dress shirt, and black pants. In a small box was a white bow tie. At the foot of my bed, there were white leather dress shoes. The suit seemed nice. I picked it up, placed it on the chair in the corner near my fireplace, and walked back to my bed.

A few moments later, someone knocked on my door.

"Come in," I looked up from where I was lying on my bed, putting my phone down.

A tanned, freckled face with bushels of auburn hair peeked through the door.

"She sent you up here to come to talk to me?"

My sister smiled, showing her mouth full of braces. "No, Rona is here because she wants to talk to you."

I could not help but shake my head at the girl.

"Rona, why must you speak in the third person? Why are you here at the Castle? You should be at Incantation School right now."

She narrowed her eyes. "I didn't go to magic school since we have a Jovial Meeting today, which you are going to."

I got up from the bed. "No, I'm not."

She snapped her fingers.

"Yes, I am."

Did I just say that? I blinked a couple of times. "You learned a mock spell?"

She smiled. "Yes, about a week ago. Now I have to learn how to get the person to *do* what they say."

She scooted closer toward the edge of the bed. "May I take a seat on the bed?"

I shrugged my shoulders. "Do whatever you want."

She sat down, crossing her legs. "You know it's being held at Qirar, barely three hours over the water. It won't take long to get there and back."

"You should be fine by yourself," I said.

She pressed her lips together. "You know as well as anyone that I hate being by myself."

"Well, if you get lonely, teleport back home," I spoke.

She rolled her eyes. "That would be truly lovely if I could do that type of spell. Qirar is a bit too far for a teleportation spell to work, anyway. You know that Mom is the worst flight buddy," Rona says.

I gave her a side-eye. *She is not your mom.* Not your real one anyway.

"I guess you're out of luck, Rona. Plus, I don't go to those meetings. I have not for years. Invite a friend to go with you or something."

I went back to focusing on my phone. Rona got gets off the bed and snapped snaps her fingers, and my phone disappeared. I gave her a dirty look.

She folded her arms. "I will be on a plane for at least three hours to and from Qirar. I don't know if any of the other royals my age will be there. So, I don't want to spend all that time alone," she finished with puppy dog eyes.

"Then why are you going?" I asked.

"Because my friend Celia invited me, and she is their princess. It would be rude not to go, especially since I'd I have been blowing her off at other events."

"Is she pretty?" I asked.

"I like her."

"That is not what I asked."

She grinned.

"I don't know what you find attractive. Come to the meeting, and you can judge yourself."

"Again, what does she look like?"

"Try looking her up."

As she walked to the door, she snapped her fingers, and my phone reappeared in my hands.

I smirked. "Thanks, I will."

She crossed her arms. "Shouldn't you ask her full name before you try to see what she looks like?"

I shrugged. "Maybe."

Rona rolled her eyes. "Sometimes I feel like I'm the one who's nineteen, not thirteen. Her name is Princess Arcelia Phacadé. I know you've seen her before. You can decide if she's worth the flight."

I typed her name into the search engine: *Princess Arcelia Phacadé*

I scanned through the pictures that came up, realizing that I had have seen her before, once or twice on television.

She had thick, black, kinky hair that went down her back. She was a curvy girl who probably came up to my shoulders.

Her blue eyes were amazing in contrast with her deep, chocolate skin. So, I knew she must be an Umbrian.

I smirked. "She is pretty, but I'm I am not going to that meeting."

Rona exhaled deeply. "Oh well, I tried. I'm I am going to eat lunch. Care to join me?"

I shook my head at her offer.

"Then I'll leave you with your thoughts."

She stopped midway through the door. "You've been more aggravated lately, sassy too. Is it because her birthday is coming up?"

I relaxed back on my bed. "Please go eat lunch, Rona."

Thankfully, she did not push on the subject. Rona glanced at me one more time and shut my door.

Not even a minute later, my arm glowed. I gazed at my right forearm, a symbol on the Emblem was giving off light.

An Apostle was trying to reach me. As I peered closer, the *Eye of Future* symbol was shining. It was Oracle trying to get me.

I sluggishly rolled myself off my comfortable bed.

"Let's see what you want," I mumbled to myself.

I touched the *Eye of Future* and spoke the words: *"Tunc aperientur portæ."*

A bronze portal opened in front of me. I stepped into the portal, and on the other side was an area filled with waterfalls.

The scenery seemed straight out of a painting, with soft blues and cascades of pink and purple flowers. When I was entirely on the other side, the portal closed behind me.

The ground under my feet was soft and gravelly. I walked on the smooth rocky path until I came upon four pathways.

I sucked the air through my teeth. I knew if I took the wrong path, I could be walking down it for the rest of my days.

I cupped my hands around my mouth. "Oracle!" I yelled. "Which path should I take?"

It was a few seconds before I got my response. "Take the path which can never be wrong."

Her voice sounded faint in the distance; I could not figure out where it came from even with my ears.

Luckily, I knew which path to take—the one farthest to the right of me. A request can never be wrong.

I came to the end of my chosen path, where I found a large pond and a silver-haired woman. Her slim body was facing away from me. She was wearing a deep pink, see-through tunic dress over a darker pink bodysuit. I could tell she was playing with the koi fish in the pond.

"You picked the right path," her voice was soft as she spoke.

I walked towards her. "Of course, I did."

I sat down next to her. "Why did you call me here?"

"Hello, Rodrick, nice to see you. How were your college courses this morning?"

I sucked the air through my teeth. "Hello to you too, blind lady."

She chuckled at my comment. Turning her head, she opened her eyes; faded irises stared out into the distance.

"I find that offensive, Prince Rodrick."

I rolled my eyes. "Not enough to not laugh at it."

"You are right," she said.

I watched as she took her left hand out of the water, drying it on the grass ground. "Rodrick, you have to go to the meeting tonight."

I made a face at her. "Why?"

She lifted her head to the sky. "A vision, no, many visions came to me. They..."

She blinked. "...They all had you in them. Each one ended with darkness, but..."

This usually happened whenever I talked to her; she would start but never finish a thought.

"You're not making sense, Oracle."

She snapped back to reality and tilted her head toward the water. "Oh, I am sorry."

Oracle's eyes saw a lot of pain throughout each day. There was so much bad in the world now that I couldn't blame her for how to shut off; she could be. She would call me when she felt she needed comfort.

I spoke in a softer tone. "It's okay, but why do you want me to go to the meeting?"

"I can show you," she spoke gently. "would you like to see?"

"Of course."

She lifted her hand into the air. I took hold of it.

Here goes nothing.

The time came for us to board the private jet. Rona, Riva, and I were the ones going from Diar. I walked past Riva as I got on. Rona took her seat next to mine. Riva sat two chairs in front of us.

From where we were, I could only see the top of Riva's head.

I was not there for her, anyway.

I only hoped that the flight would go went by fast. Rona jabbed me in the side.

"Rickie dear, you are not here to be in your thoughts the whole time."

I let out a breath. "Right, well, after all the begging you've done, I think I can be 'in my thoughts' all I want on this trip."

"You're right," she rolled her eyes and sat back in her chair.

"You're only coming because you are going to try and get into Celia's pants miserably."

I turned my head toward the window. "You think I would travel on a plane for three hours for one girl? Do you know how many girls I pick up on the street daily?"

"Whatever, Rodrick. Do not spread too many of your germs on my friend."

I smirked. "So, you are giving me your blessing to spread some of my germs on your friend?"

She pushed my arm. "Shut up."

CHAPTER TWO

The Palace Preliminaries

I quickly made my way into the Florence Ballroom on my way to find my mom. There was chaos everywhere I turned.

Workers were running everywhere. Maids and butlers were doing last-minute cleaning. Food was being sent left and right. Things were being moved around and set up, simply to be moved again.

In the eye of the storm, I saw my mom.

"Mom. Hey, Mom," I grabbed her attention.

She looked tired, just as I would expect.

She had been planning this year's Annual Jovial Meeting since she found out we were hosting.

The A.J.M. was one of the only times we would see most, if not all, our world leaders sitting together trying to discuss world problems in a civil matter. The keyword here was 'trying.'

A lot went into making the A.J.M. perfect. Hosting the meeting showed shows off the beauties and delicacies our country had has to offer.

"Yes, Celia, what do you need?" she asked.

"Am I still greeting the guests as they come in through the front doors, or am I greeting them from the ballroom's doors?"

She looked at me with an annoyed expression. "Arcelia, I already told you, you will be greeting our guests as they come in. Why are you asking me again?"

"Auntie Cal is going around talking about a new program change. So, I wanted to make sure that it is correct," I answered.

Her expression became further irritated. "Calandra is doing what!?"

She took a deep breath and recomposed herself. "Where is she?"

"Last I saw her, she was in the outdoor Botanical Gardens."

She rubbed her temples. "No wonder why everyone is confused about where things go."

"I can help out here if you need me to," I said.

She gave me a weary smile. "I do not want to give you trouble –"

"Mom, it will not be any trouble. I have nothing else to do but to get dressed."

Along with doing my hair and makeup, but I don't want to worry her with the details.

"All right," she said. "All I need is for you to help the workers set up the layout for the ballroom. The food will be presented out here. You know how we set our food plates. The tables will be placed near the food but leave enough space for walking."

I nodded in response.

"The doors to the meeting room should have a clear space, big enough for people to walk around and mingle."

"I get it, Mom. Find Auntie."

"Excellent. Thank you, Celia. If there is anything you cannot handle or need help with, get me," she said, walking away.

I knew today would be a long one, and I was glad I could keep myself busy until nightfall.

After I was done with the ballroom, I went to my room.

Luckily, I still had enough time left to get myself ready without rushing.

I heard faint bird screeches.

My Griffin, Lila, got out of her daybed and strolled over to me. She rubbed her head against my stomach. I brushed my hands through her creamy, tan fur and feathers.

I brushed her head lightly. "Lila, go back to bed. Mommy needs to change," I said.

I tried to gently push her away, but it was a struggle, as she was twice as heavy as me.

Finally, with a few more light pushes, she made her way back to her bed.

There was a slight knock on my door.

"Come in."

My three beauty attendants filed in. Viva, head of my makeup, spoke first. "My lady, are you ready to do your hair and makeup?"

"Yes," I responded.

Jammie and Lena followed me to the large vanity mirror. They began to brush my hair and set out various hair products.

"What would you like to have done today, Princess Arcelia?" Jammie asked.

"Something simple and elegant, please."

"Yes, my princess," they started working on my hair and makeup.

About an hour and a half later, they were done.

Viva had given me a classic bar eyeliner, light purple eyeshadow, blush, and dark purple lips, while the other two girls did my hair into a tight bun with side twists.

"Thank you, ladies."

"You are welcome, my princess," Viva said as she followed the other two ladies out the door.

After they left, I carefully placed my ball chain bhindi in the center of my forehead, along with putting all my earrings and nose rings.

I entered my vast closet to retrieve the dress I would wear. It was a long mermaid gown with a sleeveless bodice and a high round neckline. It had a racer bust composed of sheer black mesh fabric embellished with a plum-colored scroll-print pattern.

I put on the dress and heels and looked in the mirror.

"Perfect."

I said goodbye to Lila, who was sleeping, and made my way down the staircase. I checked my phone for any new messages, as I scrolled through the list, one stood out.

It was from Duchess Rona:

Rona: Hey, ready for tonight!!??

Me: Of course, glad you are coming.

Rona: Yeah, same. My Mom says this 1 is gonna be long…: –/

Me: Are they not all long: –) R u guys on your way, or r u here?

Rona: Yes, our plane is about to land in a few

Me: Who all is coming with you this time?

Rona: Me, my mom, and my brother Rodrick

I paused. Her brother, Rodrick, was coming?

A guard waited patiently at the bottom of the stairs.

I instantly sent a "See u soon" text to Rona and put my phone inside my clutch.

"Do I need help going to the front of the Palace?"

The guard bowed. "Yes, ma'am. It is a request by Queen Fayola."

Why would Mom think I needed help? I decided to ask her later about it. I joined him, and we made our way to the front doors. About ten minutes after arriving, people began to pour in.

My feet ached in my heels from standing so long. I was so busy worrying about my feet; I did not even notice when the Purcills arrived.

"Arcelia!" I saw Rona give me a small wave as they got closer.

I waved back. "Hey Ro," I said.

I gave her a hug when they finally reached the door at the top of the steps.

I bowed. "Good Evening, Queen Riva."

The woman forced a smile. "Hello," I twisted to face the last person, Rodrick.

I would be lying if I said I did not think Rodrick was gorgeous. Any person could say the same. His long, red, wavy hair was pulled back into a beautiful sleek bun. His skin was flawless, and his sapphire eyes sparkled beautifully. His suit framed his build and height perfectly, and he smelled of fresh mint.

"Hello," I said to him.

He glanced up and gave me a small. "Hey."

Man, his voice was excellent, too, especially that accent. They were the last to arrive, and so we headed inside to the ballroom.

Once everyone was introduced, they made their way to the bottom of the magnificent staircase.

My mom and Auntie Cal went came and stood at the very top of the stairs. My mom stood a bit further back behind Auntie Calandra. Mom was wearing an indigo gown with lace and a high collar. Her black locks were wrapped under a matching headdress. She was glowing up there. The only jewelry she was wearing was an array of earrings in her ears. Auntie Cal was wearing a gold bhindi and a gold crown with rubies. Her dress was orange, red, and golden gown. Her auburn locks were in a sizeable intricate braid going down her back.

Aunt Cal was holding a microphone and began to speak:

"Hello? Hello? Good, this thing works. Can I have your attention, please?" Everyone stopped to pay attention to her.

"Thank you all for coming to the sixty-eighth Annual Jovial Meeting! It is a delightful experience for both my sister and me to be hosting this year. In about fifteen minutes or so, all the leaders and representatives will make their way to the doors located behind you."

She gestured to the large ivory doors.

"As for the rest of your young, wonderful faces, you will be left here to mingle. We want you guys to feel at home."

She smiled. "Then again, not too much at home. We do want you to leave at some point." Some chuckled at her attempt at humor.

"On my left are the dishes and beverages. They all have name plaques. So please," she paused. "If you are allergic to shrimp, do not eat the food that reads 'shrimp pasta' on it," This time, she laughed with the crowd.

"If anyone has any questions, please direct them to my niece, Princess Arcelia." Aunt Cal guided her hand toward me. I raised my hand for everyone to see.

"If you cannot find her, the guards or other royal staff will be happy to assist you, as well."

Aunt Cal ended her announcement with a quick thank you and made her way down the stairs with my mom following behind her.

The World Spoke as One

As we all filed into the spacious meeting room, I found the seat with my nameplate in front of it.

Shortly after everyone had taken their seats, adjusted their mics, and so on, the meeting began.

"Everyone," Fayola started. "Thank you for coming. As you have been informed, we are having this meeting early this year, by request."

Her eyes shifted to me. "Made by Queen Riva of Diar, from the continent of Eruais." All eyes moved to me.

"Thank you, Queen Fayola. Yes, I called this meeting, with the purpose being…" I tapped the tablet in front of me. A dozen pictures and graphs projected to the center of the table for everyone to see. "…to discuss recent spikes in global terrorism and armed rebellion."

I pressed the tablet screen.

The screen split with a map of the world on one side and the pictures on the other. The world map had red blinking dots on individual cities and countries.

"As you can see, the red dots indicate where the highest levels of activity are: Chaparrals, Lomar, Kedaele, The Sa—"

"If I may interrupt."

I glared at Empress Jade Chartreuse of the High Court. The Empress was a leader who seemed to always have something negative to add to the equation. If her opinion was heard, it did not matter to her what others thought.

Jade's gaze was cold and gauging. "What are you trying to convey?"

"If I was not interrupted, I was leading up to my theory. I believe the cause of these events is the Atar," I said sternly.

Whispers traveled around the room. Calandra spoke. "All right, let her finish."

Jade started. "It's has been sixteen years since the Demon King's death; why are people around the globe only now trying to reconstruct—"

"Queen Riva, let me ask you this," I turned my head to see Queen Misrah of The Sanguine Palisades. Her permanent scowl was etched on her hardened face.

"What are you planning to do if this is a new era of the Atar?" she asked.

Before I could answer, Emperor Vilas of Crilima spoke up. "We all know what she, or may I have said, who she is planning on using."

"So, Queen Riva," Jade said. "What are you planning on doing?"

I narrowed my eyes. "For one, I will not be associating Prince Rodrick with this affair—"

"Queen Riva," Fayola spoke up. "Your son has the Emblem of Tempus, one of the four Deorumars' marks. He is directly involved with this matter."

"I agree with Queen Fayola," Calandra responded. "groups like the Atar prey on the beings and relics as powerful as Prince Rodrick. The mark bearers may be like demigods, but they are still vulnerable. If we were to use Prince Rodrick–"

"Understandable," I said. "Then again, no one remembers the provisions we have put in place in case something like this reoccurs?"

Others threw conjectures left and right. A Sanikin gavel thumped on the table a couple of times.

Everyone paused, glancing at King Muriell of Kedaele. He released the shadow made Sanikin, and it reverted to its normal state on the table.

King Muriell was one of the younger rulers, and through his actions, you could tell. Quick and to the point, and he found no pleasure in sugar coding anything.

"Thank you for your attention. Ladies and gentlemen, we had sixteen years to prepare. You want to tell me like Queen Riva has expressed, that none of you have been preparing for something like this to happen again?" he asked.

"We do remember the provisions we have set; King Muriell and Prince Rodrick have always played a part in them," Queen Jade frowned. "So why the sudden change, Queen Riva?"

I tightened my jaw, ignoring her. I gazed across the room.

My eyes went over to Queen Le Mai of the Ruling Lands of Xau.

"Queen Le Mai, if I may ask your perspective?"

At the age of ninety–two, she was the oldest of all the world leaders. Everyone saw her as a respectable queen and woman of vast knowledge and skill. She led her country through depression, war and drought, and all. All while keeping a level head and a strong heart.

When she spoke, all listened.

"It is obvious that this will be my last Annual Jovial Meeting. In a month, I will no longer be the Queen of my country. My grandson, Len Cirilo, will be taking over the throne."

No one spoke.

"I have witnessed, throughout my decades of rule, what the paranoia and fast conclusions of one person can do to millions of others. We should know how to take on this problem headfirst without using the child as our first defense plan. Do we believe our main source of protection should be a nineteen–year–old boy? He should not be used as leverage. Does his life have such little meaning? To speak of the Child of a God—"

"I understand that," Empress Jade started. "The fact of the matter is—"

"The fact of the matter is you interrupted me, Empress Jade." Queen Le Mai glared at Jade with slanting eyes, at once silencing her.

"Thank you. Most of us have a person in our lives that we love and care for. Most of us even have children."

She scowled at Jade, who herself had three kids. "Are you willing to use them as a weapon? Rodrick should be the very last resort to any threat this new Atar may embody.

The old woman clasped her hands together. "I have reigned for sixty–eight years, and I am telling you as a mother, the last thing I would want to do would be to use my son as a 'weapon of destruction,'" she said, glaring into the souls of everyone there.

Before anyone could say anything, a guard burst through the doors. The two guards are keeping watch on the men guarding the entrance.

"Please, please!" he begged. "I need to tell the Queen something, please! I need to, please!"

Fayola spoke. "You may speak. Quickly."

He bobbed his head. "Thank you. I was informed by a fellow guard in Diar that there was an attack on the Castle by the Demon King."

The commotion began to rise in the room. Fayola's own makeshift gavel hit the table.

"Please, everyone stays in your seat. I do not want panic to reach the rest of the guests. No one leaves the Palace until we know it is to do so. We must keep this to ourselves and our trusted personnel until we fully know the extent of the situation."

Everyone agreed with staying in the conference room while they made his or her phone calls.

"Sir," Calandra spoke this time. "When were you notified of this information?"

"Just now. One of the Castle guards of Diar contacted me," he said.

My eyebrows furrowed. "Are you aware of who I am?"

He bowed. "Yes, Queen Riva."

"You said that in *my* country, one of *my* guards called a 'friend' before notifying the queen of the country of this "attack"?"

The guard in question spoke. "No, the cell towers are down."

"How did you get your information then? By carrier pigeon?" Calandra asked.

He panicked. "No. I got the message a few hours ago."

I rose from my seat and glanced at everyone. "How much longer do you want to listen to these lies?"

"They are not lies; Ryton and his army are on their way!" A guard came to take him out, but the man had other plans. He pulled a knife out and stabbed the guard. Screams rang out. The man tried to escape, but Sanikins pulled his empty hand behind his back, forcing the man to the ground. Two other guards had come to finish the job. The man tried his hardest to wiggle out of the hold, but to no avail.

"It does not matter!" he yelled.

"He is already here! RYTON IS HERE. YOU HEAR ME!? RYTON WILL RISE! RYTON WILL RISE AGAIN! RYTON WILL RISE AGAIN! RYTON WILL RISE AGAIN!"

Everyone stared at him in shock.

I peered at the door to see that others were getting curious about the commotion and were beginning to spill into the room.

"Rodrick" was the only sound I was able to voice.

CHAPTER THREE

Royal Introductions

"Arcelia."

I turned around, smiling. "Hi, Rona."

She was wearing a strapless, pale peach gown that fell to her knees with matching strap heels. Her curly hair was straightened and curled at the tips.

I've always loved being at the A.J.M and still found myself busy with things to do. Or I was catching up with old friends, like Rona.

"I'm sorry I wasn't able to properly introduce you," she said, motioning to the man next to her. "but this is my older brother, Rodrick."

"Sup," he said.

I raised an eyebrow. "I know that isn't how you say hello to other royals."

"Oh, my bad, *amada*."

"My name is not Amada," I stated.

He gave me a smug look. "I know that."

Rona nudged his side. "I think you should stop being rude."

He smirked. "I think Princess Arcelia should learn that other people speak different languages before she tries to sound smart."

I gave myself a mental slap on the head; he spoke another language, Porta to be exact. Still, I would not give him the satisfaction of thinking he had one-upped me.

I pressed my lips together. "Funny coming from someone who cannot even correctly pronounce the R in his own name, *Hodrick*."

He chuckled. "Well—"

Rona cut in. "Be nice, Rodrick. Arcelia is the only reason you are here. I would not want to get her mad."

He scowled at his sister; she smiled back sweetly.

"I'm going to leave you two alone to better get acquainted." Rona moved to take her to leave before adding. "Bye, Arcelia. Be nice, Rodrick."

"I'm the only reason you're here?" I asked.

He placed his hands in his pockets. "she said that because I told her that you're pretty."

He's not wrong there.

"You think I'm pretty?"

"I think a lot of girls are pretty."

I rolled my eyes. "Not surprising. Have you eaten anything?"

"No."

"You are not hungry?"

He shook his head. "I don't want to be here."

"What does that have to do with you eating?"

He looked at me. "I don't want to be here or eat here."

I shook my head. *Man, he was demanding.* Who would not want food?

"If you want, I can take you to an open balcony."

He stared at me. "Really?"

"Of course. It is what I do when I am in a place I do not want to be. I go searching for escape routes."

Rodrick cocked an eyebrow. "You sneak out?"

I gave a sly smile. "I will show you where we can go after we've eaten."

After we ate, I did a bit of convincing with the guards, and we made our way to a balcony outside of the ballroom.

As I stepped outside, the frigid air quickly hit me.

"Not used to the cold, Princess?"

I pouted. "You live near mountains, Rodrick. Do not tease me about being cold."

"Aww, I didn't mean to hurt your feelings."

"You can sprout some wings and fly back home now, Rodrick," I said, crossing my arms.

"I can't fly," he told me.

I glimpsed at the horizon. "Why not?"

"Well, for one, it's too windy. My wings are light, so the wind mustn't be blowing too hard, or else it could damage them. Not all Drakonians are born with durable wings or wings at all, especially if you're not pure blood," Rodrick answered.

He leaned on the balcony railing.

"Guess you'll have to stay here and keep me company," I said, making my way to join him near the railing.

I gazed at the sky. It was dark, yet the stars appeared as if they were drawings on canvas. The moon glistened in the dark with the stars dancing around her. It was quite a beautiful sight to see.

"The sky is gorgeous, is it not?" I asked.

"It is," he responded.

"Sometimes, I wish I could join the rest of the stars up there. Hey, can you fly?" he asked.

"Yes, I can fly," I tilted my head toward him. "Why do you ask?"

He put his hands in his pockets. "Just curious."

He stared at me for a second.

"What is wrong?" I asked.

"You're shaking." Oh. I didn't notice that I was that cold.

I gave him a small smile. "I think we should go in."

"I don't want to go back inside that ballroom. Too many spoiled brats for my liking."

Like he was not one of them.

I rubbed my arms. "Who says we were going back there?"

Getting Along Well

Arcelia decided it would be best if we wandered the halls of the Palace together. It was not the best idea, but it beat the ballroom by a long shot.

"How do you like Qirar?" she asked.

"It is all right," I replied.

She glanced at me. "Care to explain?"

I focused on the wall's colorful paintings. "It is a lovely place, but you cannot give much input, being locked up in the Palace. This cannot be the only thing your country has to offer?"

She sent a slight grin my way. "It seems that you may have to come back and let me give you a proper tour of Qirar."

I smiled back. "You should, but while we're here, we could start with the Palace bedrooms–"

"It would be nice to have the Purcill Family visit Qirar. I don't remember seeing your brother Prince Rayden or your other sister, Princess Rahima, coming here," she batted her eyelashes.

I shook my head. *I guess I won't be having any real fun tonight.*

"Ray and Rahima don't have time to visit other countries."

She glanced my way. "Is it because of their kids?"

I scoff. "What do you think?"

That was somewhat the case, but not entirely it.

"I think, unlike you, I get along well with my relatives."

"We get along well enough."

"That's not what Rona tells me," she proclaimed.

I turned to her. "She gets along with people differently than I do."

She shrugged. "Hey, I would kill to have siblings. It would be so much fun visiting them in different cities."

"You can visit different countries, Arcelia. Your family rules about half of the planet."

"That is not true. It is only three countries."

"Out of fifteen, that is—" I was cut off by the sound of her phone ringing.

"Excuse me," she took it out of her purse.

She made a face at the flash on the screen of whoever was calling.

She answered. "Hello, Mom, what is—" she stopped talking.

I could hear her mom on the other side. Judging by the expression on Arcelia's face, whatever it was, it was not good. I listened to her speaking in Linga:

"Ingabe nawe nge Rodrick?"

"Yes, I'm with him."

"Kuyinto everything kulungile nawe ezimbili?"

"Okay, Mom. Is everything all right? What's the matter?"

"Okay, mina udinga ukuba Mthathe ngokwakho ukuthi kuseduze ekamelweni ukwethuka."

"What? Why do we have to go there?"

"Sicela ne hamba, mina kuningi ngizobe ukukwazisa uma ufika khona."

"Okay. Yes, ma'am. No more questions. We'll start heading there now."

"Ungakwenza hanlde lokhu?"

"Yes, I can handle it."

"Ngiyakuthanda. Bye."

"Okay, love you, bye."

She hung up, breathed, and looked at me with worry. Was she in trouble because she left?

"We have to leave."

I gave her a questioning look. "Okay?"

Before I could turn to head back to the ballroom, she grabbed my wrist. My eyes met hers.

"We're not going back to the ballroom."

Hide Me in Darkness

I found myself following Arcelia to wherever we were going. I wanted to ask her; however, something told me that it would be best to wait until we stopped. When we finally did, we were in front of a large painting.

My face deadpanned. "You dragged me to a painting?"

She spoke. "My mom wants us to stay in a panic room for the time being."

That took me back. "She wants us to do what?"

"Rodrick. I'm simply doing what my mom asks me to do."

She pressed her palm into the center of the painting. A screen glowed over her fingers. There was a soft "ding."

The painting split into two pieces, and the doors opened on either side of Arcelia. Inside was an elevator. Arcelia pressed the top button twice and the bottom button once. The doors opened for us.

She took a deep breath and stepped inside, twisting to face me. "Please get in."

I stared at it for a moment before hesitantly stepping into the elevator. She stepped towards the buttons that numbered the floor levels. She typed in a code: *4. 5. 4. 6. 3. 4. 3. 4. 5.* She pressed the "close door" button, and we began to move. The ceiling of the elevator was glass, so I could see what was happening as we descended. Above me, the painting closed itself back up again, hiding our presence from anyone outside.

We said nothing to each other the whole ride. Arcelia had her back to me. Her body language showed that she was tense with the entire situation. That did not help to shake off the growing anxiety that was starting to surface in me.

I eyed the top of the elevator, watching us dive deeper into darkness.

CHAPTER FOUR

The Light in The Dark

We finally reached our stop on the elevator. The door gradually opened, and Arcelia stepped out.

As she walked out, she glanced over her shoulder. "Rodrick, this is it, come on."

I followed her out.

There was a short flight of stairs leading to a door. We got to the door, and she pressed the code to open it.

"Press that for me, please," I pressed the switch next to my shoulder, looking up to see the roof move forward and cover the place we came in from. Arcelia got the door open, and we went inside.

We walked into what seemed to be a spacious, dimly lit room. There were two vast cabinets at the back and on either side of the room. I stood between the two cabinets, a window, and a mounted TV. The rest of the room was set up like a typical sitting room. The room's layout included a chaise longue, a sofa, and two large glass tables in the middle of the two seats. *This must be for only brief threats or emergencies.*

Arcelia moved over to the wall nearest to us.

"What are you looking for?"

"The light switch."

"Why?"

She huffed. "Rodrick, it is pitch black in here."

How could she not see–*Oh*!

I went over to her and turned on the light switch. "I forgot I could see in the dark. My bad."

She beamed. "It's cool."

She paused. "Wait, you can see in the dark?"

I chuckled at her surprise. "Drakonians can."

She took a seat. "You learn something new every day."

I shook my head and took off my suit jacket, placing it on the sofa.

"Do you know how long we'll be here?" I asked.

"My mom says about an hour."

I eyeballed the room until I spotted a clock. It was 10:30 PM,

"Okay, so how are we to know exactly when we can leave?"

She walked over to one of the glass tables.

"There's an intercom system we use," she replied, placing a small wireless intercom on the table.

"Once I turn it on, we'll be able to talk to whoever has the mobile part of the intercom upstairs. My mom will contact us first," she said.

"Okay, what are we to do until then?" I asked as I laid back on the sofa.

"I have no clue."

I gave a dry laugh. "So, we're going to stare at each other for an hour, Princess?"

She sucked her teeth. "I do not hear you coming up with any ideas, Prince Rodrick."

I groaned in annoyance. "Don't call me that."

She grinned. "What? Don't you like your title? Would you rather me call you, Duke?"

"Stop it."

She laughed. "You look adorable when you're pouting."

I crossed my arms. "I'm not pouting."

"If you say so," she whispered.

I rolled my eyes.

"Rodrick, I have a question."

I tilted my head in her direction. "Ask away."

"How many tattoos do you have?"

"Twelve. Why?" I asked.

"I've seen the pictures, and Rona talks about them."

"Of course, she does."

She smiled. "Rodrick, how old are you?"

"Nineteen."

Arcelia gave a slight "oh" face and sound, then went back to silence.

"Why did you ask my age?"

She shrugged. "I thought you were older."

"Really?"

She bites her lip. "You said you had twelve tattoos; that's a lot for anyone, especially for someone your age."

She should tell that to my two older siblings. Rahima has more than twenty-five, and Ray beat her out with his thirty-six and counting.

"You're eighteen or nineteen, right?" I questioned.

She pushed back some of her long, curly hair back into its bun. "Yes, I'm eighteen."

"Do you want any of your own?" I asked. "Tattoos, I mean."

She hummed. "Yes, I do. I don't know what I would get. I'm thinking of putting my first one on my upper arm."

First one?

"How many tattoos do you want?"

She picked at her nails. "I want, uh, maybe about six or seven."

Whoa. That was surprising. Few princesses, with the exclusion of my sister Rah, have or wanted tattoos. Let alone *six* of them.

"What, I surprised you?" she asked me.

"Yeah, you did."

She pressed her lips together. "Rodrick, doesn't Rahima have an arm and leg sleeve?"

I crossed my arms. "She doesn't count."

She laughed at me. "Why not?"

"I don't count my family as typical royalty."

She raised an eyebrow. "You would count my family as *typical*?"

She had a point. Her mom and aunt were the first-ever sisters to rule over the two parts of Qirar. Qirar was a country of voted royalty, so it was a surprise when both Queen Fayola and Calandra won the elective votes. Fayola in the Northern region and Calandra in the Southern. Qirar was a bit off from the rest of the world with its ruling system, but it was one of the oldest rulings and legal systems in the world's history. Many things that occurred there had been happening for hundreds of years. That included the ruling of the upper and lower regions of the country by two separate persons. Oddly, though, the two monarchs lived together in the center of Qirar—another one of their weird rules.

Meanwhile, Arcelia's other aunt, Sultana Ephedra-Rosanna, lived and ruled in the Siesa Arid's capital city, Hupogee, the largest underground city. Sultana Ephedra also had twin daughters that both had a form of Schizophrenia.

And Arcelia's older cousin, King Muriell, had an arranged marriage with his wife, Queen Naline, to end the war between their countries, Kedaele and Sevoelle.

Still, that doesn't compare to having a brother who was a drug addict and married a maid with three kids. A sister with bipolar disease and another sister who was adopted due to "public appearance standards."

"You have a point," I said. "and a lot of facial piercings."

She smiled. "So, you've noticed."

"I used to want more and got obsessed with what I would get, but I opted for this," I pointed to a single ear-piercing.

She walked over and took a seat next to me. "You could get more."

She peered over my face, shaking her head. "Nope. Your face is too good for piercings."

I laughed. "So is yours."

She smiled. "I know, except it is an Umbrian tradition."

"Really?"

She picked at her fingers again. "Each piercing has a meaning, purpose, and status. The bhindi too, but it's just not rammed into most Umbrian's heads."

Wait, most?

"So, how many piercings do you have?"

"I think ten."

"Ten?"

"Yes…ten."

"So, where are they?" I asked curiously.

"I have three on each ear. A helix ring in my right ear. On my left, a tragus ring. My nose piercing, eyebrow piercing, a septum ring, and I have my belly button ring."

I studied her face. "Did you need to poke that many holes in your body?"

She playfully rolled her eyes. "Yes, Rodrick. As I said, they all have significance."

The intercom began to go off. I examined the clock, 10:55, not too long of a wait.

Arcelia walked to it and answered. "Hello, Mom?"

"Hello dear, how are you and Prince Rodrick?"

She rotated slightly toward me. "We're fine. Why are we here? Did something bad happen at the A.J.M.?"

The Queen let out a small sigh. "I'm sorry I have to rush and confuse you like this. We had an altercation in the conference room with a man impersonating a Royal Guard. The man claimed to be a follower of the Demon King."

My eyes widened. "What!?"

I could not be hearing her right. *Ryton the Demon King?*

The visions from Oracle flood my mind: *blood, scars, fire, and dead bodies. Too many to count.*

Queen Fayola's voice snapped me back into reality. "He claimed that Ryton is planning on rising again. I do not know what your knowledge of this man is or his actions, but this also ties to why I want you to go with the prince. I want you both to get out of the country."

Arcelia looked at me just as surprised. "What? Mom you–"

"Honey, with everything that has been happening in the world this past year, I do not want to take any chances. Especially when we are discussing an uprising with Ryton."

"Can we not just go somewhere else in Qirar?"

"If they can infiltrate our security system, then nowhere in Qirar is safe for you."

"But—"

"Arcelia, no arguments. We do not have time for this."

Arcelia went silent.

"Prince Rodrick are you close by?" the Queen asked.

I stood up and moved next to Arcelia. "I'm here."

"Good, I know you can handle yourself well in a situation like this, correct?"

"I am."

"All right, your mother and sister are on their way back to Diar," she said.

"Thank you, Queen Fayola."

"You are welcome. I will continue to stay in contact with you both, and Arcelia will know-how. I do not know how long you will be gone but know that if this is Ryton truly coming back into play, he is after you."

I kept silent, watching Arcelia.

"We will further investigate the events going on of the A.J.M. before and after the attack. Please keep hidden and safe until I notify and approve both of you to come back."

"Okay," she whispered.

"I'll have a guard sent to escort you both."

"Thanks," I replied.

"You are welcome. Take care of each other."

"Love you, Mom. Bye."

"Love you too, dear. Let the eyes of the Gods watch over you both." With that, she hung up.

"I need to sit." Arcelia took a seat on the sofa. "Guess now we wait."

"Arcelia—"

"Rodrick, please. I need a moment," I respected her wishes and closed my mouth. I sat down and laid my head back again.

Soon there was a knock on the door.

I looked up from where I sat across from Arcelia. She stood up and opened the door.

A single guard stood on the other side.

"Come on, Rodrick, time to go."

I got up and glanced at what the guard was holding. They were two sizeable travel-size duffle bags.

"These have clothes and toiletries for you," The man said.

"How did you know my size?'

"You wear a large?"

"No. Extra-large," I said.

"Guess you will have to squeeze."

I grimaced.

"I'm happy to change out of this dress and these heels. They're killing me."

I glanced at her feet. "Why did you not take your heels off?"

She gawked at me. " Take what off? In what universe—"

"Princess, could we please continue this discussion on our way to the vehicle?" The guard inquired, cutting her off.

She rolled her eyes. "Lead the way."

Shortly afterward, we arrived at the back of the Palace; there were three more guards behind an all-black SUV. They took our things and loaded them into the back of the truck. The guard who was with us left after Arcelia and I got into the car. There were five guards in total. Two sat in the front. Arcelia and I sat between two more, and in the third row, the last guard was behind me. After everyone was seated, we moved.

I glanced at the princess. "You know where we are going?"

Arcelia looked at me. "It should take about thirty minutes from here."

I tried to relax, but in my gut, something felt off.

A couple of minutes went by before Arcelia spoke. "Excuse me, sir, you're going the wrong way," The guards looked to the front.

The driver looked at us briefly in his rear-view mirror. "No. I take a different route," he pronounced in a thick Sanguinarian accent.

"All right," Arcelia replied suspiciously.

The car was silent again.

The SUV made its way onto a dirt road off the main path. Arcelia gripped my hand.

I watched her face, and she looked at mine.

Something was not right.

"Você fala Porta?" I asked her.

"I understand some," Arcelia replied in a whisper.

"Você sabe para onde estamos indo?"

She shook her head. "No."

"Speak Anglish so we may understand you," I glared at the guard sitting next to me.

"No, por que eu deveria?" I said back.

"I said to speak Anglish. We do not understand Porta, your Highness," the guard answered through gritted teeth.

"Why must we?" Arcelia questioned.

"We simply want to be informed of what you speak," he said back.

"Why do you think we did not speak Anglish?" I shot back.

The eyes of the driver were on us again, but he was silent.

"I do not think you know where we are supposed to be going," Arcelia said.

"I know. I take a different route—"

"I do not care if you take a different route; we should have been there by now."

She looked at me, then the driver.

"Stop the car."

"I cannot do that."

Arcelia turned back to the guard who spoke. "Are you the one driving? No? Okay, then."

She glared at the driver. "Stop the car."

He continued to drive.

She gripped my hand harder. "Rodrick."

I clenched my jaw; these people were not royal guards.

Arcelia raised her empty hand.

A shadow casting from the steering wheel was followed, wrapping itself around the wheel and pulling back. Another shadow headed for the pedals of the car. The car jerked violently, finally coming to a stop.

Through the commotion in the car, I saw a glimmer of silver from the guard up front, aiming at us. He threw what was in his hand. I caught it—a knife.

The guard behind us wrapped his arm around Arcelia's neck. She released her bonds on the shadow at the wheel. The driver slammed on the gas pedal. My fist grazed the guard's chin next to me. Arcelia head-butted the guard behind her. I wrestled the guard next to me in the small space. The driver yelled as another arm grabbed me by the neck. I gripped the head of the man behind me and slammed it onto the inside of the car multiple times.

I launched a kick at the man in front of me, this time to his ribs. He cried out. The car began to steer to the right. The cold wind brushed my face. I turned my head to see Arcelia had pressed the guard's neck into a slightly open window. A fist landed in my lower stomach, then two blows to my ribcage. Fighting past the pain in my gut and ribs, I fended the guy off with a kick to his face. The man behind came back again, throwing a haymaker. I ducked as he hit the other guard instead.

The car began to swerve and turn more. I heard cracks in tree branches around us. The car picked up more speed. The front of the car came to a rough stop, colliding with something before flipping.

All I could hear was Arcelia's scream.

CHAPTER FIVE

UNWANTED HOMECOMING

I remembered talking to a few of the other guests at the A.J.M. when suddenly we all heard a painful scream coming from behind the ivory doors.

A man shouted. "RYTON WILL RISE!" repeatedly.

I headed toward the door with the rest of the crowd. Once they were opened, we spilled inside. There was a man restrained in the far corner surrounded by a small puddle of blood.

Queen Fayola was trying to get everyone to stay calm.

While Queen Calandra tried to push us out of the conference room, world leaders paid no attention to either of them as they made calls on their phones.

The hectic scene hit me hard.

Where was Rodrick? I saw him earlier with Arcelia. I looked around for them. Nothing. They were not in the room. With all the noise being made in there, they could not be in the ballroom.

I tried to search for another familiar face, my mom. I saw her and pushed toward her. I tried to ask her questions. "What happened? Why was there a guard getting escorted by other guards out of the room? Where are Arcelia and Rodrick?"

She looked at me. Her face showed no emotion. As if someone had come along and pulled her plug. That was when everything became a blur. Suddenly, everyone was quiet. People headed out of the room. Mom took hold of me and went towards the door.

Was Rodrick safe? Was he in danger of something?

The questions flowed through my head. A headache started to form.

Before I could blink, we were on the jet headed back home.

The plane ride home was silent due to Rodrick not being present.

It was a rush, and I had no time to process everything that had happened within the last few hours.

Mom had a phone attached to her ear for most of the ride. I sat and watched her as the questions continued to pile in my head.

Once she got off the phone, she met my long gaze.

"Rahima and Rayden will be at the Castle sometime after we come back."

As if my mind was not filled with enough questions already.

"Rodrick is safe," she monotoned.

I looked away from her and gazed out the window. Her eyes never strayed from me. Once we landed, we were driven back to the castle in a hurry. Mom still had a phone pulled up to her ear—this time for the whole ride.

When we got back, my head was pounding. Mom seemed to notice and told me to go to bed.

I opened my mouth to say something, but she beat me to it. "All of your questions will be answered once you have had a good rest. Okay?"

I bobbed my head hopelessly. "Okay. Goodnight."

I headed up to my room when I heard her voice responding in the distance. "Sweet dreams, Rona."

CHAPTER SIX

THE GIFT OF A GOD

I screamed, opening my eyes.

I was moving, but everything around me wasn't. Well, they were. Just…slowly. Everything was at a snail's pace, if at all that fast.

"Arcelia."

I turned, looking at Rodrick. His irises, golden, his right arm shining.

"You, okay?" he questioned.

I gawked at him. *What was this?*

"It's all right; I'm the one doing this," he said, reassuring me.

The windshield was cracking. The glass shards glimmered in the air. Each of the men was readied and braced for impact. The hood and front of the SUV were mangled and breaking apart. It was as if Rodrick had pressed pause on the whole accident.

I realized he was holding my hand as he started to tug. "We've got to go. Come on."

I slowly followed him through the side window of the car.

The car was in mid-flip. None of the men moved or reacted to our leaving. The truck was heading into the trees and bushes.

"Rodrick, what did you do?"

"I'm the Acolyte of Time," he said as if it were that simple.

"Oohhh," I gave myself a mental slap. *How could I have forgotten?* Now everything around, us made sense.

I eyed the slowly flipping truck.

"What do we do with them?" I asked, pointing to the guards. "We can't leave them there."

"Can you use some shadow puppets to get them out?" Rodrick asked. "I can't do much of anything in this state."

"I can, and they are called *Sanikins*," I distorted the shadows nearest to me into five large vines, pushing them into the car to pull out the five men. As I did, Rodrick worked to get our bags out.

I got the men out and placed them on the roadside. They were in shock. I could not tell if they were aware of what was happening.

I combined my Sanikins to create two large hands, grab the car and place it carefully back onto the road.

Rodrick peered at the men. "Should we leave them like this?"

I used a shadow to strip them of their belts, wrapping and knotting them around their hands while fastening them together.

"I think they're good now."

He let out a breath. "Do you know how to get us out of here?"

"Yes, get into the passenger's seat," I slid into the driver's seat and waited for him.

"Can I drive while we are so slowed down?"

He exhaled. "No. I wasn't holding onto the car when I slowed everything down."

I peered around at the distorted scene around us. So, that was why he was holding my hand.

"All right, can you turn it off? I need to see if the car will even drive."

His eyes gave a yellow glow before reverting to their lovely, original blue.

Everything moved again. After a few tries, the car engine caught. I spun us around and carefully drove down the road, praying to the Gods that the car would hold up until we got there.

"Okay, where is this thing supposed to take us?" Rodrick asked.

"To Waeven," I said, making a sharp right turn.

The Waves to Waeven

Arcelia turned off the car. "Okay, this is our stop."

I shifted in my seat. "Really?"

We finally reached our stop. We were off a back road in front of a small old shed. She got out. We got our things, and I followed her to the shed's door.

She typed in the door's code and pushed it open. We entered the shed, where we found another elevator. We began to descend below the ground again. The elevator doors slowly opened again after a few moments. Arcelia stepped out. As she does, she peered over her shoulder and spoke to me. "Rodrick, this is our final stop."

I began to follow her out, walking into what seemed to be a garage. On my right was a giant black submarine. The rest of the space was quite empty.

I looked back at the sub. *This was how we were going to get to Boscages of Waeven.*

"Now, to answer your question," she mounted the submarine. "This is how we are getting to Waeven."

"I kind of figured that out," I said.

She scoffed. "A simple 'okay' would have been better."

I shrugged as she made her way up the submarine's ladder. When she reached the top, she, yet again, logged in to another password. The head of the sub creaked as she used shadow puppets to twist it open. When the lid was fully accessible, she got her bag.

"Do I have to tell you that it is now time to enter the sub, or did the big boy figure that out already, too?"

I bit my tongue, picked up my things, and followed her into the sub.

"Oh, before you follow along, please, if you could, close the sub's door hatch behind you. Thanks."

I closed the lid and climbed down the ladder; the smell of dead fish and sea salt hit me. "Gosh, it stinks in here."

She gave me a slight glance. "Rodrick, what is an underwater boat supposed to smell like? Fresh flowers?"

I stepped onto the sub's elevated floor. "No, but at least put in some air fresheners."

"You say that like I visit this place every weekend," she said.

"So," I looked around. "Where do I put my stuff?"

Her lips pressed together. "If you had kindly waited a few more seconds, I was going to give you a tour of the place."

I gave her a sly smile. "That doesn't answer my question."

"I'll be showing you where to put your things and where you can sleep," she answered over her shoulder.

I shook my head and followed behind her. She took me all over the sub and explained where the bathrooms, control room, and sleeping quarters were situated. The sub was separated into two floors and two halves. The first floor's front half held the deck passageway, mess hall, and a small gallery. The second floor's front half was where the beds, bathrooms, and control room were. While the back top and bottom halves had the boiler room and engine, among other things. After the tour finished, she took me to the control room.

"Okay," she said. "this, if you didn't read the sign, is the control room."

She pointed to a medium-sized screen located in the center of the control panel. "This lovely screen here is our GPS. We'll need to take shifts to make sure we're going in the right direction."

"Should the sub not already know?" I was puzzled.

"The sub isn't that updated," she said quickly. "It should work well enough to get us from point A to point B, hopefully without any mishaps."

"So, if this thing is to sink?"

"We have lifeboats and jackets," she snapped.

I could tell she was annoyed, but this was our life we're talking about.

"Is there a problem?" I asked.

Her blue eyes stared at me with heavy eyelids. "No, I'm fine. Only tired. You mind taking the first shift for the thing?"

"You mean the GPS?" I corrected her.

She nodded slowly. "Yes."

Her accent sounded stronger, probably because she was tired. Her perfect bun seemed to be spilling out of itself. Beads of sweat covered her arms and face. Her dress seemed to press to her curved body rather than accentuate it. She embodied the term "worn out."

"No, I don't mind."

She rubbed her face and eyes. "Thank you. I'm sorry I have to put you through this, but when we get to Waeven, I'll be asking my mom about all of this mess."

"I should be the one apologizing, not you."

I had the urge to ask her how she was going to contact her mom. She had placed her phone in a "no service" containment box earlier and made me do the same.

"How long is my shift?" I inquired softly.

"About three hours, then you can get—"

I cut her off. "How long is it to Waeven?"

Her hands hung limply by her side. "About seven hours."

"I'll stay up for the seven; I can sleep when we get there. If I need anything, I'll come and bother you."

She stared at me in shock. "I…Thanks. Really," she gave me a faint smile.

I moved my head toward the door, telling her to leave. "Goodnight, Princess."

She walked past me, a soft smile on her lips.

"Goodnight, Rodrick."

Rise and Shine

I woke up to banging on my door. "Arcelia, we have 20 minutes to reach Waeven; get up!"

My eyes shot open.

20 minutes!

I need about four more hours of sleep and one hour to get ready!

I groaned. "Rodrick, I take like a 30-minute shower—"

"Well, I guess you should hurry. Now get your stuff together because the sub isn't going to wait on you."

I rolled my eyes. He talks as if he knew where we're going.

I swung my legs over the bed and rushed to get myself ready.

Quickly, I made my way to the closest bathroom and locked the door. Once I was done, I looked at the mirror in the bathroom. I looked like a hot mess. Well, a cute hot lot. My eyes still had small bags under them. My hair, due to the humidity, looked like a static bear. I wasn't wearing a drop of makeup, which did not bother me as much as my hair did. I laughed at myself and pulled my hair back into the most decent afro-puff I could do. I wore dark gray shorts, a black shirt, and dark-colored steel toe boots.

I heard Rodrick's voice again. "We have five minutes," I made my way out of the bathroom and into the control room. Rodrick was leaning back in a chair.

"You ate breakfast?"

He twisted his face. "No, mom, I did not eat breakfast. As if I would eat anything on this piece of crap."

Well, it seems someone else needs to sleep too.

Abruptly, a ping sound came from a flashing red light on the dashboard next to the GPS.

A minute later, the sub came to a complete stop.

Well, we're at Waeven.

Rodrick and I quietly gathered our belongings and made our way out of the sub. Once we were out, we were in a garage, like the one back home. Inside was an old, deep-gray SUV with tinted windows. After throwing his things into the open trunk of the truck, Rodrick went inside.

Placing my things in the back, I also got in. I started the car and pressed a button on the dashboard. The wall on the opposite side of where the sub was, pushed out slightly and slid to the left side. There was now an exit for us to drive out. As we got closer to the door, I zoomed up the incline and out the sub-port.

I pointed to the same button on the dashboard. "Please press that," I said to Rodrick.

He did as he was told without speaking, which was nice for a change. The exit became shrouded, hidden in plain sight once again.

The ride was again quiet. I looked at Rodrick. His eyes were unfocused and glossed over. He was tired. His right arm was supporting his head. He had let his crimson hair down. It fell gracefully around his shoulders while the wind pushed it onto his face. He wore a white tank, which lightly hugged to his very muscled torso.

I swear he looks—

"Arcelia!"

I turned back to the road and slammed on the breaks. We both jerked forward, hard.

I had almost hit a tree. I looked over at him.

He sneered. "You drive like my brother. Try looking at the road more than you do at me."

I mumbled an apology and got back on the road.

I look at the truck's control panel. *Hey, it has an Auto Drive mode!*

I gladly pressed the button. "Ha, Rodrick, now I can stare at you all I want."

"Is that so," I froze.

Crap.

I said that out loud. I turned to Rodrick, who had a sly grin on his face.

"I didn't mean to—"

"What's been said can't be taken back," he said, cutting me off.

"Shut up."

"Why didn't you put the car on auto before?" he asked.

I gave a sheepish grin. "I didn't know it had one."

"This is why we pay attention," he said back. I gave him some serious side-eye and turned to the driver's seat window.

The Boscages of Waeven had beautiful rainforests. The lush greens of the trees and foliage resembled ancient fortresses that stood proudly above us. The sweet smells of flowers and fauna lingered throughout the area. The colors, the animals, and the constant rainfall were all scenic to me. It made everything feel safe and calming.

"Hey, Arcelia…hey, wake up. The truck stopped."

I felt Rodrick nudge me softly. I woke up groggy, looking at him. He pointed to the front of the SUV. It stopped upon a rocky mountain slope.

"Oh, I know where we are—"

"I would hope so," he jeered.

I rolled my eyes and got out of the truck. I went to the slab obstruction. I felt around for the hidden lever. I felt Rodrick's confused gaze on me.

"I'm looking for a switch," I answered. I heard the car door slam and Rodrick walking next to me. He, too, started to feel around for the lever. A few moments later, I found the cloaked switch.

"I found it."

Rodrick stopped searching. I turned the handle clockwise twice then counterclockwise once. A part of the wall slid open to the left of me. I told Rodrick to follow me back to the truck. I moved the car forward into the vast cave. The air felt damp.

As we entered, the opening behind us started to slowly close. The headlights switched on as we continued down the dark pathway. We reached the end of the path. I exited the car and turned to Rodrick. "Go get your stuff."

He looked at me. "Why can't you get it? You have two arms," I gave a smug look. "So, do you."

"But they're tired," I rolled my eyes and mumbled under my breath. I got my things, leaving his. Eventually, he got out and went ahead to get his stuff as well.

"Now, what?"

Gosh, I hope he's only this annoying because he's tired.

I pressed my hand to the wall in front of me. It scanned my hand, and a staircase pushed out of the wall. Thankfully, it was lighted to the top. I turned around toward Rodrick. "After you," he went ahead. I went to turn the car off and followed behind. I headed up the stairs. At the top was a door. Rodrick turned to me, like a small pleading child, pointing at the pin pad.

"4859."

He quickly pressed in the numbers and pushed through the door. I followed him inside.

Before he could say anything, I spoke. "The bed."

I pointed to the bed resting at the corner of the room.

"I'll give you a rundown of everything once you've slept. Okay?" he gave me a slight nod and made his way over to the bed.

I placed my stuff down next to the coffee table and then turned back to look at Rodrick.

He had removed his shoe, socks and now was working on his shirt. *Stop staring, stop staring, stop staring, stop staring, stop staring.*

I quickly made my way to the kitchen area of the room before Rodrick could notice I was ogling him. Again.

I heard a creaking noise came from the bed, letting me know that he was in it. I breathed out.

From a cupboard, I got out a Meal Ready-to-Eat, roast pork. I finished eating, threw my container away, and went to the sofa to get in my lost hours of sleep.

Bunker Away from Home

My eyes opened. I was sitting on the ground. I stood up to see a narrow path in front of me. I made my way down the road. My right arm began to hurt.

I was used to it, giving me trouble, though this time, the pain was a lot greater than in the past.

Someone echoed my name. "Rodrick...Rodrick..."

I could not see them; however, the voice was familiar.

A flashing light appeared at the end of the path.

"Rodrick...Rodrick...come follow..." the voice teased me.

I continued to walk until the path came to a stop.

There again were two ivory doors standing before me. I cautiously pushed them open.

The same light reappeared.

"Rodrick..."

Where did I know that voice from?

I did not reach out for the light this time. It did not seem to matter since the light transported me again.

I found my gaze drawn to a temple.

The pain in my arm continued to grow.

I grabbed my arm, eyeing the temple. The gold and white paint were peeling off, and the pillars were barely holding up.

I walked up the uneven stairs to the front of the fading building until I was back on the path I started on.

Now a staircase with the Emblem at the top loomed before me.

I heard that familiar voice. "He will rise. Rodrick, run. He will find you. Run, run, baby boy."

My eyes widened; only one person called me that.

Maia.

The only true mom I ever had.

The path vanished at my feet.

I needed to get closer.

Her voice grew louder and more daunting. "He will rise. You shall fall. He will rise. You shall fall."

The ache in my arm rose.

It throbbed all over my arm and twitched in my fingers.

If I could only get closer.

If I could only reach the Emblem.

This would all go away; it had to.

Finally, I reached the Emblem and grabbed it. But, instead of the Emblem in my grasp, it was another hand.

Maia's hand.

Her starving frame stood meekly. Her golden hair was tied in a messy bun, and her maid's uniform was torn and worn.

My heart began to race as if it was trying to leave my body. I clutched my chest and felt it pounding against my hand.

She spoke. "If you could not save me, you will not save them."

She let go of me.

The stairs disappeared as I fell into the dark abyss.

I could still see her face. Her tanned skin was dusted with freckles. Her sunken cheeks. Her big olive eyes.

I heard her voice. "Rodrick!"

It grew louder the further I fell.

"Rodrick!"

Stop. Please. Stop.

"Rodrick, Rodrick, Rodrick, RODRICK!"

I tried calling her, yet no sound came out.

No!

Please, Maia! I tried to save you.

I could not see anything as my vision blurred.

"You cannot save them if you too want to save yourself."

I woke up sweating. My body was heating up, and my heart was racing.

I rotated to study where I was in the bunker with Arcelia. I saw her asleep on a sofa.

My stomach growled. It's been hours since I last ate a full meal.

I wanted to let Arcelia sleep, but my stomach was begging for food. And I needed to get my mind off that terrible dream I just had.

I walked over to her with weary legs.

Her limbs were spread all over the satin sheets on the sofa's frame. Her chest slowly rose and fell.

I tugged her arm. "Arcelia. Arcelia, wake up."

Her face twisted a bit, but she did not wake up. I tugged on her arm some more.

She finally opened her eyes, and her blue irises looked up at me.

"Rodrick," her accent was intense. "what do you—"

She stopped. "You're shirtless."

I snickered. She turned her head away from me, hiding her face.

"Arcelia, it is okay to look at me. I will not bite. Unless you want me to."

She eyed me. "Did you need something?"

I held my empty stomach. "I'm hungry."

She slung her smooth, chocolate legs off the sofa and stood up. "Let's fix that, so I can go back to sleep."

She moved past me toward the area behind the sofa.

I had not noticed how small the place was until now. The walls and floors were the color of dark wood. A sofa and a coffee table sat in the center of the room. There were small round windows dotted around the room, along with fake plants. Right in front of the door was the tiny bed I had slept in. Above it was a small wall clock. Behind the sofa was what looked like the kitchen. It consisted of a top and bottom cabinets, a sink, and a corner table with two chairs. To the left of the living room was the bathroom. It had a large tub and shower with thick curtains, a closet door, and a vanity sink with a mirror. The closet door seemed to be where the toilet was hidden. Finally, in the far corner of the bunker was a small desk.

"If we're supposed to be hiding, why are there so many windows?" I questioned.

"The windows are for me," she answered.

I looked at Arcelia to explain more.

"It's like how you need water to live, but if you consume too much water, you can get over hydrated. Sunlight causes my body to balance the casting of shadows and darkness, so it does not consume me."

"So, if there is too much sunlight…."

"…It can harm me too," she finished my sentence. "Are you coming to eat?"

I stretched out my arms. "I am. I was only scanning the place. So where are we again?"

"In the Boscages of Waeven," she replied, smiling as she turned away from me.

I sucked in a breath of air.

"I meant where in Waeven are we?" I asked as I walked over to her.

"We're in the Fishing District of Waeven, about a couple of miles away from it. Then about a 20-minute drive from the capital city," she said.

"So, what do you want to eat?" she asked.

I peered down at her. "What is there to eat?"

"We only have MREs."

"MREs?" I twisted my face; whatever they were, MREs did not sound appetizing.

"Yes, Meals Ready to Eat. You've never heard of them?"

I shook my head.

She grinned. "Well, there is a first for everything."

She pulled out some MREs and placed them on the countertop. "Qirar used to only use them to feed soldiers in the military, but it got popular with civilians. Mainly because it does not require electricity to cook the food. Everything inside of the meal is listed on the front of the packet. I put out lunch ones since it's late afternoon now."

Late afternoon?

I had forgotten we got here in the early morning. What surprised me the most was the fact I had slept that long.

"Are there instructions?" I questioned.

"Yes, on the back. If you need help—"

"I will ask you. Thanks."

She nodded.

Arcelia looked like she wanted to say more but was avoiding it. She eyed me, and I looked down. I had forgotten that I was still not wearing a shirt.

I snickered.

"You can look down, Princess. I don't mind," I said as I winked.

"I'd rather not," she shuffled her feet. "You should put on a shirt."

"You would stare at me with one on too."

She frowned and began to walk away. "Shut up, please."

I watched her hips sway as she made her way to the desk. I forced my attention back on what I wanted to eat.

Hmm, chili and macaroni, ratatouille, vegetarian lasagna, and spaghetti and meatballs. I decided to go with chili and macaroni.

The only food I recognized was the chili, so it seemed like the safest bet.

I placed the other meals back in their cupboard and started preparing my food.

When I finished 'cooking,' I made my way over to Arcelia. She was writing on a piece of paper.

"What are you writing?" I asked.

She didn't take her eyes off the paper. "I am writing to my mom. Since I'm too restless to go back to sleep now."

The paper appeared old and crumbled. "How are you planning on getting the letter to her?"

She stopped writing and looked at me. "This paper is different. You write down what you want, crumble the paper, and blow it out the window."

I stared at her, confused.

"When crumbled, the paper turns into petals. You blow the petals away. The paper flows to the person on the receiving end."

"Okay. So, it's kind of like a bird messenger."

"Yes. It's called a Bract Epistle Tree. Umbrians used this way of messaging as opposed to homing pigeons."

I took a bite of my meal. "So, what happens when the petals come back?"

"They file into one of those branches," she pointed to the small pot on the desk with a wooden tree statue in it.

"They revert into a piece of paper when they touch one of the tree's branches."

"How long will it take for the letter to get to her and her response back to us?" I asked.

"For it to go to her and back, only a couple of hours, a day if the weather is bad," she answered.

"So, what are you writing?"

She moved her hand to better show me the paper. "Can you read it?"

The letter was in Linga. I shook my head. "No."

She hummed. "Well, it says: 'Hello Mom. Prince Rodrick and I have made it safely to the bunker. Is everything going well? Do you know how long we will be here? Please let us know if anything comes up.' I am going to write more, but that's what I have so far. Is there anything you want me to add?"

I bit my bottom lip. "Yes, can you ask if my sister and Riva are, okay?"

She began to write again. She reread the letter and crumpled the paper, softly blowing on the petals. They lifted off her hands and out the small window above the desk. They danced along in a thin line toward their destination.

Arcelia got up and moved to the sofa, patting the seat next to her. I walked over and joined her on the couch, eating my chili and mac.

The chili wasn't the best, but it was better than nothing.

"Rodrick?"

I stuffed my face with the food. "Yes?"

"If you don't mind me asking, why did you call your mom by her first name?"

I continued eating. "Because she is not my mom."

"She's not?" she eyed me with surprise.

"She's the woman that gave birth to me. That is as close of a bond we have together."

"Oh," she whispered.

I finished the rest of my meal.

"Sorry for asking."

I shrugged. "Don't take it to heart. It is fine."

She bit her lip. "Okay, if you'll excuse me, I'm now going back to sleep."

I turned my head to the princess. "Why? You got like twelve hours already."

She grinned. "Umbrians need at least ten hours of sleep, but I need at least sixteen."

I raised my eyebrow. "Really?"

"Yup. I am drained too."

I rolled my eyes. *What was she tired of?*

"Do you guys need ten hours of sleep?"

She gave me a sheepish grin. "We would not have enough power or energy to make Sanikins or control our other abilities like phasing or shadow cloaking. Umbrians work best at night, so most of us do not start our days until 1:00 pm."

I shook my head. "I need a good four hours of sleep, and I'm straight."

She yawned.

"Are you that exhausted?"

She shook her head. "No. I need to do something to keep me busy, or I'll be sleepy and sluggish."

Her eyes leisurely slid over to my right arm.

"Do you want to look at them?"

Her head perked up. "Really?"

I scratched the back of my neck. "I don't mind."

She moved closer to me. "Can I touch them?"

I gave her a slight nod. "Be my guest."

Every girl I met always wanted to touch my tattoos. As if they would move when connected. Her soft hands grace my arm. She handled every spot on my arm with such delicacy. I saw how fixed her stare was on every tattoo.

She stopped and looked at me. "I only counted ten; I thought you had more."

I twisted around so my back was facing her. "I only have ten on my arm."

"I cannot believe I didn't see this one," she gently pressed her hand onto my back.

"They're beautiful."

I closed my eyes, relaxing with the movement of her hands. "Thank you."

She traced the lines of the tattoos softly with her fingers.

"The wings are so detailed," she circled the center of my back. "The mandala is amazing too."

She glided her hand over the two words on my shoulders.

"Divine, Calamity," she whispered, moving her hands away as I turned back around.

"How did you count ten tattoos on my arm? I only have nine."

She pointed to the forearm, gliding her fingers over the Emblem of Tempus. "This one made ten."

I shook my head. "No, this is the Emblem of Tempus."

Her eyes sparkled. "Really? It's gorgeous."

She was correct; the Emblem was a work of beauty.

The mark was gold and bronze with hints of burgundy. At the very top of the mark was a blazing sun. At the bottom was a crescent moon with stars.

But the middle was the actual attraction. The Circle of the Apostles was made up of three circular rims. In the second and third rims were four symbols, each standing for one of the seasons.

Arcelia smiled. "The Gods know how to be made very beautiful things."

I looked at her. *They sure do.*

Her hands left my arm. "I have one last question."

"Okay, what?"

"Can you please put on a shirt?"

I chuckled and got up. "Nope, it's too hot."

CHAPTER SEVEN

A Few Unanswered Questions

The whole family was assembled, except for Rodrick. Ray, Rahima, Mom, and I sat silently in one of the Castle's many reading rooms.

Rayden, my oldest brother, was leaning back in one of the chairs. I had not physically seen him for a while, but he appeared healthier than ever. He seemed to be getting more body mass onto his lean frame. It appeared that he had gotten more neck tattoos too. His hair was braided down his back, and his beard had finally filled in. He wore a denim jacket, dark jeans, a juniper green V-neck, and black boots. His soft blue eyes were slowly wandering around the room.

Rahima, the oldest of us, was sitting on the other side of the room. Her legs were crossed, and her hands clasped together. Her long ruby hair was pulled out of her face, so you could see her big blue eyes and faint freckles. Rah's wedding ring gleamed in the light of the room. She was wearing a blush floral blouse and a pair of heels. Her gray skirt did little help to cover her leg tattoos.

Mom was sitting in front of me. Her hair was straightened and in a half-bun. She was wearing a cobalt sweater dress with black heeled boots. Her face showed no emotion; her eyes held no spark.

For a few minutes, everyone was still.

I decided to break the silence. "May I ask my questions now?"

Rah looked at me. "Go ahead, Rona."

I thanked her. "I have a lot, so bear with me, please."

Everyone hummed in response.

"All right, where is Rodrick? Is he okay? What happened at the meeting? Why did we have to leave so quickly?"

Before I could ask any more questions, Ray interjected. "Okay, Ro. Let us answer those first before we continue."

"Sure," I said.

I noticed Ray's and Rah's eyes shift to Mom. She got the "message" and turned to me.

"Rodrick is fine, from what I know. He is in the Boscages of Waeven, hiding. He is under the watch of Princess Arcelia, who escorted him there."

Her voice was faint, but her demeanor was icy. "A threat appeared at the A.J.M. It seemed to be about the Atar's new uprising."

I focused on her, processing the things she was saying.

"The terrorist attacks that have been happening, are they connected?" I questioned.

She eyed me. "Yes, and I believe Ryton is coming back."

Ryton?

My eyes darted between Ray and Rahima. "He was the king—I mean your dad."

Rahima shook her head.

Ray spoke up. "That monster is not my father. He has not been for sixteen years."

I peered over at Mom. "How could he be coming back? I thought he committed suicide in prison last year."

Mom crossed her arms. "We did not want any commotion after we found out that he escaped from Prison Astria. That is what I and a handful of world leaders decided to go with to the press."

I was in shock. "So, until now, you have not captured him?"

"No. To this day, we have been searching for him," Rahima stated.

"So, he is still trying to kill Rodrick?" I asked.

What if he already...

"Rona."

"Yes, Mother?"

"What do you know of Ryton?"

"I know he was the king of this country years ago. I know he wanted the world to be equal or whatever. So, he tried to force it to happen. He made the Atar, which made him crazy in the head, and he tried to kill Rodrick. He ended up in jail and died about a year ago," I looked at everyone.

"Darling, that is not precisely what happened," Rahima said.

My head shot up. *Then what was the truth?*

"Wait, Rodrick is, okay? Right? You said he—"

"Rona, we told you, he is fine," Mom said.

The room fell silent.

"So," Ray sat up in his chair. "Are you going to tell her what happened now? Because we are on a tight schedule, Riva."

Mom gave him a sharp look. "My title to you is Mother."

She directed her attention to me. "Rona, what I am about to tell you will not leave the walls of this room. Understood?"

"Yes, ma'am."

"Good."

WEAK WARRIORS

The dirt path on which we traveled seemed to spread out for thousands of miles. We had been walking on foot for about twenty-five minutes. The weather was hot and sticky. The bugs buzzed all around us, unwanted company on our journey. Even so, I could not complain too much about Amarem's spring weather. It was much more unforgivable in the summer, even for a Drakonian.

I took my machete and lashed through the thick vines and trees.

"Sir?"

I turned my head to the left. "What is it, Chanton?"

"Some of the men are wondering when we will reach the gates."

I paid no attention to Chanton as I cut through the lush greenery. "If they feel they want to turn back, they can. You should not waste my time telling me such insignificant things."

"Sir, we have been on foot for at least an hour."

I rolled my eyes at his exaggeration and continued my path.

"Demon King, I said that we have—"

"I heard you," I cut him off. "and I do not care if they want to go back; they can."

"Are we not almost there?"

I paused, giving him a menacing scowl. "I will cut off your tongue if—"

An arrow sliced through the air, landing near my foot. I looked in front of me.

Through the shrubbery, I made out a tall woman. I grinned wildly. I lifted my hand and burned through the remaining wall of green separating us. I stepped through the flames. The woman stood in front of Vrata Za Žene's gated doors. She had braids going down her back and was wearing a black tribal dress with armor over it. Her caramel skin was tight, and her brown eyes were piercing with determination. I felt the feeling of superiority that radiated from her. Above and around her were more women in battle gear, staring down at my men and myself.

I shook my head. *Perfect, just as I intended.*

"Galian," I said, raising my voice. "How lovely to see you again."

Her eyes slanted. "Ryton. Leave now."

"All I want to do is speak to your mother," I said. I knew my tone would taunt her.

She pointed a dual-bladed staff at me. "You will only be leaving here. Last warning."

Her people readied their weapons. Various arrowheads, spears, and swords pointed at us.

How foolish of her. Brave. But very foolish.

I stabbed my machete deep into the ground.

Giving a dark laugh, I withdrew Mithril from her scabbard. "You should hear yourself. Pathetic."

I twisted toward my troops. "Men, here are our two objectives: Get through the door..."

I let my scale layer sprout from my body, covering my skin entirely.

I spun back to Galian. "...and kill as many as you can."

I cleared through fifteen of their sad excuses for warriors in no time. One by one, the women fell. Their weapons were mediocre, and their fighting skills were pathetic. *I knew toddlers who fought better.* I could have done this blindfolded and still killed as many already.

All their bows, spears, and arrows could never compete with my sword, Mithril. We easily could have used guns and ended it quickly, but where's the fun in that?

I made my way toward my intended target.

Galian stood her grounds at the gate.

Her weapon ready at hand. "This is the end of the line for you. Last stop."

I gave her a wicked smile.

Our blades locked. She was quick to pull back and move. Our bodies swung across the area. She charged at me with force, but I quickly blocked her and followed with a backswing.

She dodged, but I met her with another strike. The weight of the hit sent her staff free from her hands.

I smirked. "Stop now, and I will not place your head on that staff."

She smiled back. "I do not give up that easily," she drew Khopesh swords from her back. "No talk. We finish this."

I scowled.

Now I was over it. "I wish you would stop wasting my time."

She charged at me, striking twice. The first missed, but the second sliced the fabric of my shoulder.

Time to finish this.

I drove my blade at her, barely missing her neck as she dodged. She and I clashed blades three more times.

The fourth time found her flesh.

Blood gushed from her waist.

I leered. "What a lovely shade of red."

She gripped her wound, visibly becoming angrier as she bolted toward me. Our blades jarred against each other once more. She pressed her weight against her sword into me, causing our weapons to interlock.

"What a weak woman," I taunted.

"I am strong. I show no fear in battle," she said.

I glanced behind her, smiling. "No, you do not...."

A sword impaled through her back and out of her chest. She dropped her weapons. The bloodstain spread over the rest of her chest.

"...but you do show weakness."

From behind, Chanton pulled his sword out of her body.

Before she could fall, I caught her by the braids. "More of your people's blood will be spilled due to your nerve."

I dropped her dying body, rolling her over with my foot, cleaning my sword as I did so. I turned and looked around me. Bodies and blood covered the once green and lush grounds.

Most of the women were dead or were retreating behind the gates.

I grinned.

"Men," I turned to the gates. "Shall we?"

"Oh," I pointed to Galian with my sword. "Bring this body with us."

I made my way through the crowds of crying women to the Pagoda. We made our way up the steps and past their sorrowful tears. The doors of the Pagoda slowly opened before us. I let my men go before me.

They tossed Galian's body at the feet of their ruler and her mother, Bellona. She rushed down from her throne. I stepped in her way, pointing my sword at her daughter's lifeless body.

"Ah-ah-ah. No touching."

I glared down at the foolish elderly woman. "Not until you give me what I want."

"Why," she pleaded. "You cannot have the Tempus pieces. Please, you already took my daughter—"

"I will not hesitate to take more lives if you want to continue this." I spat back.

She kneeled at her daughter's body; tears poured from her face,

"Ryton, you will kill us all."

"That is the plan if I do not get what I want."

I so desperately wanted to slice her body in two. "I will start by taking your head back as a souvenir."

Her eyes shone with resilience.

How idiotic.

"I will not hesitate, Bellona," I said, stepping closer, the end of Mithril inches away from her neck.

"I cannot let my daughter's life be for nothing."

Scowling, I grazed Mithril along her neck. "You are wasting your breath. Give me the pieces."

Her eyes gave me an answer.

I smiled. "Very well, if you insist."

I propelled my sword into her throat. Blood spilled out of her mouth. Screams around me rang out.

I slid out Mithril, swung it through her neck, separating her head from her body. I watched her decapitated head roll on the glossy floor. I turned my attention to the other sobbing and fearful women.

"Now, who wants to get me my pieces?"

UNWANTED GUEST

The doors to my private alcove slid open. I walked in and headed to the drink cabinet. I pulled out a bottle of aged whiskey and grabbed a glass of ice. I set the glass and bottle onto my desk. I walked around the desk to the grand picture placed behind it.

It was of an angel standing among countless dead bodies. In its left hand was a blood-seethed dagger, and in the other, a white dove inside a golden cage. I opened the left side of the picture's frame to reveal a hidden lock. I spun the lock and went ahead to open it.

Inside held the Crest of Time. It was round and gold in color. No more significant than a serving tray, but no smaller than a dining plate. The fragile pieces of the Crest bonded together with thin rays of light.

I pushed my hand into my jacket pocket, pulling out a small bag. I took six pieces out of the bag and carefully placed them onto the rest of the Crest. As I put the pieces in their rightful spot, they formed a gold seal between each other. I finished placing all six pieces. I stood back. Six pieces down, five more to go.

"You have outdone yourself, Ryton."

It had been 17 months since I left prison. I said left because I did not have to escape. It was simply a matter of waiting for the right moment.

I let the world think I killed myself while I was at Prison Astria. Why? To set my plan in motion, of course. Now was the perfect time for me to step back into the light. Riva and the others were foolish to think the connections I had would disappear once I was put in prison.

I felt the first time around I was in the public eye too much to see and know. It was both a blessing and a curse. I gained many loyal subjects and just as many opposers.

When the time came for me to go to trial, I had the Crest collected pieces, I had the Time Spear, and Rodrick was only three years old. I was so close, but my ego and pride ended my success before it had even begun.

Still, after all these years, I was able to get everything back on track. There was only one significant difference between the past and present. Rodrick.

The little boy was now a grown man. It had been a sign from the Gods when the boy was born. He was my gift. The proof that I was to lead Earth into a new era. They gave me Rodrick. They gave me the Acolyte of Time. Tempus gave me a blessing.

Even though I had to plan to make sure that Rodrick would be the next Acolyte, it worked in my favor.

I was destined to have this. It was my fate and the future of the world. My blood would be my key to this world's salvation.

One child would be used to liberate billions of lives. And it was supposed to be all under my watch.

I should have captured him and dealt with Riva's "wrath" later, but I had no time to raise a child.

So, as always, I left it to Riva. But I was unconcerned.

It would be harder now to get him to follow me, but I can do it by force. I had been in the shadows watching and learning. My army was growing bigger and bigger—day by day, year by year. I am confident, and nothing will stop me from getting what I want this time. I chuckled.

The Zona Kingdom learned that lesson.

The sound of my intercom went off, ruining my moment of accomplishment. I sneered. I pressed the answer button. "Quickly."

"Sir, there is a guard here who has information on the Qirar emissary."

I massaged the bridge of my nose. "Let them through."

A minute later, the guard entered my study.

He bowed. "Demon King."

I finally sat in my chair.

I grabbed my lonesome whiskey, pouring myself a glass. "You have five minutes of my time."

I side-eyed him. "Do not waste it."

"Yes, sir," he took a breath. "We were notified of the Qirar situation. My emissary is in the custody of the Royal Guard. We–"

"Did he complete his mission?" I demanded, swirling my glass of alcohol.

The guard gulped. "No sir, but—"

"He was to notify the rest of you if the Key was in the area. Then you were to move in and oversee the rest of the assignment. If he did not find the Key, he was to come back and tell of his findings. Seeing that you said he is in the authorities, he must have done something of great disorder. Yes?"

The imprudent man nodded.

"Why is he in custody, and do we know where the Key is?"

Beads of sweat rolled down his face. "He was apprehended due to making comments about your rising, the placement of a weapon on his person, and stabbing a guard."

I eyed the man in front of me.

"Th-the Alpha squad were able to disguise as Royal guards and obtain access to the vehicle he would be in. But…it was unsuccessful."

I could smell the fear seeping from him. "Do we have the Key?"

His body started to tremble.

I rose from my chair. "Do. We. Have. The. Key?"

He swallowed. "No."

"Do we know where he is?"

"…No."

I protracted my claws, carefully picking up my glass, and finished it.

I swirled what little ice was left with a clawed finger.

"I give him one job. A job only meant for no longer than an hour. A job that a seven-year-old brat could do better than him."

The man's lip began to quiver.

"For extra measure," I stared at the melting ice. "I sent a group of men with him. Somehow all of you were able to mess this up."

"The Key is not alone, my King. He is with Princess Arcelia—"

I shot him a threatening glare. "Was I not speaking?"

He closed his mouth. How dare he interrupt me.

I paused, and I placed the glass on the table. "Why am I now just hearing of this? The A.J.M. was a day ago."

"We were not notified of the situation until–"

"Everybody in that meeting left. Including the Key?"

"Y-yes," The words tumbled from his mouth.

I shook my head. "You have wasted my five minutes."

I smashed the glass onto the table, propelling what remained of it at the man. Shards of glass speared into his hand. He cried out in pain as he sunk to the floor, gripping his bloody hand. I walked over and grabbed him by the neck, flinging him against the door. I adjusted my posture and retracted my claws.

"Get out."

The useless being scampered out of the room.

I walked back over to my desk, and I pressed the intercom button.

"Send someone to clean up the mess in here."

"Yes, Demon King."

"Oh, and that useless excuse of a Human that is about to walk out, send him to the laceration room."

"Yes, sir."

Bits of dirty blood and glass stained my hand.

Men have such revolting colored blood.

I stopped looking at my hand and pondered what the man had confirmed.

They know I am alive. Rodrick is with Princess Arcelia. I peered back at the intercom.

Let's play to their fear.

I pressed the speaker switch. "Direct me to the weapons room."

"Yes, sir."

A moment later, the cleaning lady appeared. I told her to wait outside. She did as she was told and left.

"Hello, Demon King," the voice on the intercom said. "It is a pleasure to be hearing from you."

I smirked. "Of course, it is, General Maves."

I walked around the desk. "I need you to make a short visit to Diar's Castle."

"So, soon?" he inquired.

"Yes, I have been notified that we are going to have to start earlier due to another setback."

"When would you like me to go, sir?"

I walked back over to my desk and sat down.

"Tomorrow afternoon."

"Yes, sir. Do you have in mind what you want me to be doing?"

"Yes, I do."

My intercom went off again. I glanced at it. *Who was bothering me now?*

"General, I will discuss more with you later."

"Yes, my King. I look forward to our next conversation."

I hung up.

I answered the pending call. "What is it you want?"

"..."

"Hello?"

"Hello, Demon King."

I jumped back with my claws ready. I lowered my hands when I saw who it was.

She was wearing a black cloak with deep purple designs at the hem. The hood was lowered to make her face visible.

Her jet–black hair was slicked back in a ponytail. Her pure white skin glowed in the light, along with the lilac Calavera makeup she was wearing.

"To what do I owe the pleasure to be greeted by Lady Death?"

She stood mute, her violet eyes staring me down.

"At least take off your cloak."

I guided my hand over to my empty coat rack. "It can become quite hot in this room."

She glided her way over to the coat rack. "Is the heat in here coming from you, or did you not pay your AC bill?"

I chuckled.

Under her cloak were a velvet dress and black heels. Black opera gloves covered her hands. However, there was no sign of her scythe.

"If you did not come here to kill me," I moved around my seat. "then why are you here?"

Her violet eyes met my green ones. "I came here to warn you," she proclaimed as she seated herself.

"Oh, warn me of what, Lulonah?"

She scowled; I smiled.

"Do you know how many women you killed today?"

I sucked my teeth. "You did not answer my question."

I moved to pour a new glass of whiskey.

"Care for some?"

"I do not drink."

"You should," I took a swig of my glass.

Her eyes hardened. "Ryton. Do you know how many innocent people you slaughtered today?"

No, and I do not care.

"Innocent people do not carry weapons on their backs," I spoke.

I placed my glass down on a nearby surface. "Those women's lives were meaningless. Therefore, it does not matter to me how much harder I do your job. I would have warned you, but there is no way for me to contact you."

She remained silent.

"As a matter of fact, you should be thanking me," I picked up my glass again. "I did give you some more work to do. To keep you busy."

"I did not need 'more work.' What made you think I would be happy about this? You did this for fun. This was not out of defense or protection."

I smirked. "Killing by defense or protection, is ok with Lady Death? I thought you hated ill-death in any form."

"Not anymore."

I looked at her with intrigue. "Oh?"

"We are off-topic."

"We are only starting an interesting conversation."

"You are going to die, Ryton. That is what I came here to tell you."

I huffed. "And who is going to kill me? You?"

She appeared in front of me; her right glove was off. "If I could kill you right now, I would. All it takes is one touch with my hand, and you are gone. But I won't be the one to get that pleasure."

I licked my lips. "My death would give you pleasure?"

She lowered her hand from my face. "No, it would give me resolve."

I grinned. "Well, I cannot have that happening, can I?"

CHAPTER EIGHT

FAMILY ONLY IN PUBLIC

Ray, Rahima, and I sat in silence as we ate our lunch. I only picked at my food. After what Mom had told me about Ryton, I did not have much of an appetite.

"Are you not going to eat?" Rahima asked, looking at me with worry.

I twirled my fork. "I am, Rah."

Her worried expression deepened. "I know that you're worried about Rodrick, but—"

I cut her off. "Everything is fine. Nothing to stress about, right?"

She narrowed her gaze.

Ray butted in. "Rona, we aren't telling you to not worry about Rodrick. Just do not put it above everything else, okay? You have not eaten at all today. This is Rodrick we're talking about. If anything, he's probably doing better than we are here in this hellhole."

Rahima spun her head toward Ray. "Language."

Ray rolled his eyes. "I'm not five, Rah."

Rahima sucked air through her teeth and went back to eating.

I gave a little chuckle.

She started up again. "It doesn't mean you have to use that type of language, does it, Ray-Ray?"

"I'm too old for that name, Rahima."

"Then you are too young to curse."

"Rahima, I'm twenty-three. Those two things—"

"I'm twenty-seven," She snapped. "What's your point?"

They continued to go back and forth, which made the situation more comforting.

I laughed.

My two older siblings looked in my direction.

I began to eat. "I'm glad you guys are here. I'm happy to have more than one person for the company."

Rahima smiled. "We're happy to be here too."

"Indeed, but how are my nieces and nephews?" I asked.

"Are you asking Ray or both of us?" Rahima said.

"No, only you, since I clearly did not say, *nieces.*"

She sucked her teeth. "Shut up."

Ray gave a smile. "To answer your question, Ro, they are doing fine. Kick is starting to play instruments. Lala has joined a dance troop, and Am'lee is essentially going 'where the wind takes her.'"

"It seems those three are keeping you busy," Rah replied. "How is Rosanna?"

He chuckled. "That baby is running the house. Ali and I created a monster with that one."

I laughed. "Of course, she is. That's a baby's job."

The clicking of heels rang down the hallway.

We all watched as Riva made her way into the dining room. Her walk demanded attention.

How lovely—someone to "brighten" the mood.

Her hair was flowing down her back. Silver strands of hair danced in between the fading red ones. She was wearing a long lavender kimono over a khaki jumpsuit.

She eyed us with steadiness. "Is *almoço* going well?"

We agreed in silence.

Mom scanned our faces. "I heard you talking. May I ask what it was about?"

"I was wondering how my nieces and nephews are doing," I said, making eye contact.

She hated it when people talked to her without meeting her eyes. she said it showed weakness.

She sat down, something I was hoping she would not do.

"Is that so? Well, my dear, did you get a response?" she crossed her legs and looked toward her other children.

"Yes, she did," Rahima replied, annoyed.

A maid entered the dining room. "Does anyone need anything?"

Mom turned to her. "Yes, a glass of red wine."

She looked at Ray and Rahima. "Do you two want any?"

"No," They both answered.

"Does anyone need anything else?" The maid inquired.

"No, ma'am, we're fine," I said.

The maid curtsied and went to get Mom's glass of wine.

"I have told you, Rona," Mom looked at me. "you do not have to address them as 'ma'am' or 'sir,' they serve you."

Ray glared at her. "And you don't have to ask me if I want to drink. You know I don't drink."

She glanced at him. "Habits die hard."

He narrowed his eyes. "They can still be broken."

She tapped her fingers. "How are my grandchildren doing?"

Ray looked at his food. "They are fine."

Mom looked over to Rahima. "How is Cecil?"

"Fine."

The maid came back with her glass of wine. "Put it on the table."

"Yes, ma'am."

"It is Queen Riva," Mom stressed, her gaze stinging holes into the poor maid's soul.

The maid gulped. "Yes, Queen Riva. Does anyone need—"

"You are dismissed," Riva said, waving the poor girl away.

The maid timidly bowed and left.

Ray shook his head. "The Castle seems to still be as wonderful as I remember it."

Riva sipped her drink. "It is better than hiding away in the woods in some run-down mansion."

"I live near a forest, not in one. It is not the fact we live there that bothers you. You solely want everyone to live the way you think they should."

"He is not lying," Rahima stated, poking at her food.

Riva sipped her wine. "All I want is—"

"—For people to live up to your exacting standards," Ray cut in.

Mom scowled. "Do not start with this again, Rayden."

I rolled my eyes. This was playing out just like I knew it would.

Perfect.

He took a bite of his food. "Do not start what, Riva?"

"Ray, leave Mom alone," I teased. "Or do I have to call Alistine to come here?"

He laughed. "Leave my wife alone."

"Is she doing well?" I asked. I wanted us to ignore Mom's presence. I knew that was a ridiculous thing to do, but I did not want any more fighting.

"Of course, I feel I shouldn't have left her alone with four kids."

Rah beamed. "If she can manage you, she can handle those kids. Plus, she already had three before you. One more should not—"

Riva scoffed.

Ray rolled his eyes. "What now, Riva?"

"Nothing," She took a sip of her wine. "Nothing at all."

"Riva," Rayden uttered. "I want to eat my lunch in peace. I cannot do that if you are going to be throwing shade at the things we say."

She finished the rest of her wine. "Rayden, you are supposed to call me *Mãe*. Show me respect as your mother. All I have to say to you has already been saying."

"Mom, have you eaten lunch?" I tried changing the subject.

"Rona, all she consumes is alcohol and hatred," Rah huffed.

"And all you do is throw tantrums and destroy property, Rahima," Mom sneered back.

Rah narrowed her eyes. "Do not start with me, Riva."

"Start what?"

Ray got up and headed for the door. "I am going for a smoke."

Riva scoffed. "I wonder what you'll be smoking."

He stopped walking. "Riva. Shut up, will you? No one asked you to come here. No one asked you to speak. No one—"

"No one asked you to do drugs; even so, you did," She turned her head to meet his eyes.

"Riva goes burn-in—"

"Ray, please!" Rahima cut in.

Ray left without another word.

I slumped my shoulders.

Fear Blooms to Reality

The sweet sun dipped low behind the hills. The stars started to paint themselves across the sky. Arcelia loved to stargaze on these types of nights. My daughter was out there, on the other side of these stars.

What kind of mother am I? I let my only child stay with that boy while I sipped my tea, acting as if all was well.

Everyone thought Arcelia got a terrible food virus and was on bed rest. They also believed that it spread to Prince Rodrick and Duchess Rona while they were at the A.J.M.

I heard my sister's heels click as she came down the hall. "You cannot come out of your office every so often to mope around, Fay."

My body eased up. "I have nothing else to do, Calandra."

"Yes," she folded her arms. "it's not like you have to administer Northern Qirar, sign documents, plan spending budgets and kiss ugly babies."

I rolled my eyes. "That is the one task I can claim to do."

She walked up next to me. "Which one?"

"The kissing of ugly babies."

We laughed.

"Fay," Cal rested her hand on my shoulder. "She's okay."

I shrugged her handoff. "No, she is not. Arcelia is on an island with the Acolyte of Time, who the Atar and Ryton are after. Ryton will not hesitate to hurt her. I'm so stupid to think she could do this by herself."

Cal's facial expression soured. "Argue me this, why when we found those four phony guards sitting in the forest tied up, did you not decide to bring her back?"

I looked her in the eye. "At that moment, I believed that she could manage herself. I regret it now. I was reckless to think she could."

"Fayola, you think beating yourself up over your decision will make of any good?" she asked me.

I paused. "I should make her come back. I can have someone else take her place with…him. I do not trust that boy."

Cal curled her lip. "You trust his snake of a mother more?"

"Cal, please, it's rude to call Drakonians snakes."

She leaned on the window. "No, it is rude to call Serpents, snakes and Drakonians, dragons."

She grabbed my hands and squeezed them. "You felt the possibility you picked was the best one, Fay. By the hands of Vitae, Celia will be okay. Knowing that daughter of yours, she will not leave that boy alone, even if you ask her to come back."

Cal looked at me. "She is an adaptable Umbrian; she can handle herself well. Celia and the prince will—"

"My Queens, please excuse my intrusion." We both watched the Royal Guard bow before us.

"You are excused," Calandra replied.

He stood up straight, his face flushed red.

"We have been sent a message."

I narrowed my eyes. "By whom?"

"The Demon King," he answered.

My body went stiff. "What does the note say?"

The guard breathed out. "It didn't note my Queen. It was a warning of what is to come if he does not get Prince Rodrick."

"What warning?" Cal demanded.

"He attacked the Zona Kingdom and assassinated their leader Bellona and her heir, Galian. Before he left, he set the kingdom on fire."

No.

He shifted his eyes to the floor. "He killed 386 of their women."

My sister and I were speechless.

By the Gods.

CHAPTER NINE

SLEEPLESS

Since we arrived, I had not been able to get much sleep. Arcelia, on the other hand, was knocked out cold.

I laughed at the princess. Her covers on the futon were all over the place. Her body warped in the sheets. Her hair was tousled and tangled across the pillows. Comfortable. It was the best word to use to describe the way she slept. I sat back in the bed, scanning the bunker before me.

The night felt serene. Sounds of Arcelia's light snores and the creatures of the night echoed through the small space.

It was not as bad as I thought it would be. The room was airy, open, and *green.* Green because of the fake potted plants everywhere.

There was the sound of soft rain falling in the background. Small windows dotted everywhere, letting in the faint moonlight.

I studied my right forearm. The Emblem shone under the moonlight like someone had branded my inner arm with gold.

The dreams I have been having, what do they have to do with you?

I flopped back on the bed, staring at the ceiling.

"What can I do to get some sleep?" I said out loud.

Then it hit me, *Sandman.* He can help.

I checked to see if Arcelia was still sleeping. Yup, out like a light.

I can go and come back, no sweat.

I touched the *Sands of Slumber* symbol on the Emblem.

"*Tunc aperientur portæ.*"

A bronze gateway portal opened in front of me. I slipped into the portal. I entered a vast room filled with mountains and mountains of golden sand.

"Careful, Rodrick, you know that is sleeping sand."

I looked up at the dreamscape-painted ceiling. The Sandman was wearing a huge brown scarf, thick glasses, some beige wool top and pants, and floating on his back.

I cupped my hands around my mouth. "Hey, Sandy! Could you come down here for a second?"

"Sure thing."

He floated down carefully.

His feet hovered over the floor. "Are you here to talk about your strange dreams?"

"You know about them?" I asked.

He returned to floating on his back. "Rodrick, of course, I know. You are Tempus' vessel to Earth, so I get a direct stream of your dreams. They have not been this interesting in a while."

I made a face. "So, my dreams are streaming media for you?"

He adjusted the glasses on his face. "Yes. I thought you knew."

Yeah, right. You guys rarely talk to me about anything dealing with my abilities.

"I have not been able to sleep because of those dreams. I don't know what they mean. Can you tell me? Maybe that will help me sleep better," I folded my arms. "Or I can stay up all night contemplating what they mean."

At this point, I am willing to take the chance.

He played with some sand in his hand. "Rick, I cannot interpret dreams; I can only give them. If you want someone to do that, talk to one of my sisters. Oracle or Fate would be your best choice. Through Anamnesis, you can look back in on some of your memories and—"

"Sandy," I cut him off. "can I go to them now?"

He spun to float on his belly. "Nah, they're asleep."

I placed my hands on my face.

Why do demigods need sleep?

He snapped his fingers. "Hey, I can give you some sleeping sand. You can try it to see if it will work."

A trail of golden sand flowed into his left hand. With a snap of his fingers, he wrapped the sand inside a small pouch.

"Here you are, sleeping sand from the one and only Sandman."

I took the pouch from his hand.

"Just close your eyes and rub some of the sand on them. Only use a pinch at a time and no more than a pinch. If you do, you may end up in a sleep coma for days or weeks. Oh, and it does not work very well if you are having nightmares."

"Thanks," I had a gut feeling that the dreams I have been having were nightmares. All this would be useless. I guess I came here for nothing.

Sandy sulked. "Rick, I wish I could help you more. You can always talk to my siblings or something."

I shook my head. "You must not know what is happening then."

Sandy floated back to me. "What is happening?"

"It is a long story."

"Come on; we've got time," he poked.

"No, *you* have time. I need to go and sleep."

"I guess I will see you later, in your dreams," he wiggled his eyebrows.

"I—bye Sandy," I opened a portal to go back.

"Bye. Oh, wait! If you can, talk to someone about your dreams. I know it sounds boring or weird, but trust me, it'll help."

He looked at me with sincerity.

"Thanks, Sandy."

I slipped into the portal.

I was back in the bunker; everything was as I had left it. I sat back on the bed, gripping the sleeping sand in my hand. I looked out one of the windows, and the sun was breaking out from the horizon.

I kept forgetting time moved slower while I was in Taporis.

As I thought to myself, I heard a soft mumbling. Arcelia was waking up.

She stretched her legs onto the floor.

"Morning, *princesa.*"

She turned to me with sleepy eyes. "Good morning. Did you sleep well, Rodrick?"

"No."

"Was my snoring too loud?" she asked.

I shook my head. "It has nothing to do with you."

"Are you feeling well?"

"I'm fine," I got up and lay next to her on the futon.

"I'm going to take a shower," she said.

I had sunk more into the cushions. "All right."

She got up and started to get her things. She moved to the curtain that covered the shower and tub.

While she was hidden behind the curtain, my eyes wandered around the room again.

My eyes landed on one of the many fake plants. My breath hitched.

It had large, tall, green leaves with red tips and giant Hibiscus flowers.

A Poignant Hibiscus.

I remembered the plant. And I remembered how much I hated it.

Hugs and Kisses

I raced down a Castle hall.

I looked back and called out. "Mommy, hurry! We can make it outside to play. Run!"

A young maid, barely over twenty-five, ran after me. Her curly yellow hair was tied back in a bun. She had olive eyes and tan skin with lots of freckles.

"Rodrick, you know I can't run that fast. Slow down, Sweetie," she laughed as she tried to catch her breath.

"Baby boy, slow down—Achoo!"

I stopped in my tracks and turned to her. "Mommy?"

Mommy walked around a plant and sneezed.

It had big green leaves with red tips and giant flowers.

I hurried over to her. I must save Mommy!

I pushed away from the evil plant. The vase smashed on the floor. Yay! I saved Mommy! I am her hero!

Mommy grabbed my hand and pulled me away from the mess.

She quickly wiped her runny nose on her dirty uniform skirt. Her sneezing became louder.

"Rodrick—Achoo! You cannot do that. Achoo! Achoo! Now mommy has to clean—Achoo!"

I frowned. "It makes Mommy sick. It was evil, and it hurt you."

She smiled. "Yes, Mommy is allergic to the Poignant Hibiscus. Achoo! That does not mean—Achoo! I was gonna move from the plant—Achoo!"

Sad, I dropped my head down.

I made Mommy worse.

I am no hero.

"I'm sorry."

She sneezed again.

She cupped my face. "It's okay, Sweetie."

I heard someone approach us.

"Maia, I'm sorry to interrupt," It was Mrs. Erma.

She turned to me. "It is time for Prince Rodrick's training lessons."

I held on tighter to Maia's body, and she did the same.

"I don't want to go, Mrs. Erma," I looked at Mommy with sorrow. "We didn't get to play today."

Mommy wiped her nose. "Achoo! Do not worry, and we'll play later."

She cupped my hands in hers and gave them a light squeeze.

"I promise I'll still be here," She turned away, sneezing.

I gave a sad sigh.

She hugged me and whispered in my ear. "I love you. See ya soon."

I looked at her. "I love you too."

"Prince Rodrick," Mrs. Erma said. "It is time to go. Rodrick..."

"...Rodrick, Rodrick, RODRICK!" I jumped.

Arcelia was calling me.

"I've been calling your name forever. Are you okay?"

I slowly moved my head. "Yeah, I was lost in thought. My bad."

She plopped down next to me on the sofa, crossing her legs under herself. "Are you sure?"

Sandy's words popped back in my head: *"If you can, talk to someone about your dreams. I know it sounds boring or weird, but trust me, it'll help."*

"Actually...never mind."

She nudged my arm. "If you've got something on your mind, say it."

"It's okay; I'm fine."

I knew she knew I was lying, but thankfully she did not probe any further.

I shifted on the sofa. "So, what are we going to do?"

She held her nose. "First, you're going to take a shower."

I straightened my posture. "This is my natural smell. It's called morning husk. It's sexy."

She rolled her eyes. "Not to me. You stink."

I laughed, getting up. "Alright, you think of something to do while I go take a shower."

She scrunched her nose. "And brush your teeth."

I moved closer to her face. "Sssorry about the sssmeelll."

I quickly ducked before she could hit me with a sofa cushion.

After I'd brushed my teeth and showered, I made my way back to the sofa.

Arcelia went and threw away what I assumed was her breakfast.

"I know what we can do," Arcelia said as she sat back down. "You can let me do your hair."

I ran a hand through my semi-dry tresses. "Why would you want to do my hair?"

"I want to give you fishtail braids. Plus, you just washed it, so I know I won't catch anything when I touch it."

I decided to ignore her comment about her catching something from my scalp.

Well, I have nothing better to do.

I sat down on the floor between her legs.

Arcelia ran her fingers through my hair. "You have really smooth hair."

"Thank you."

She began to comb her fingers through my hair. "It reminds me of mermaid's hair."

"You mean *merman's* hair."

She laughed, massaging my scalp. "Take or leave the compliment."

"I don't see how saying I have female fish hair is a compliment."

"They're not fish. They're Mermaids."

I tilted my head. "Their lower parts are fish."

She began to braid my hair. "You have a problem with Mermaids?"

I leaned back. "No, I do not."

She clicked her tongue. "You sure? It sounds like you do."

"You're not hearing me, right."

"Really?"

"Probably," I said.

I felt her twist and tug my hair. "What are you doing?"

"I am starting over. I didn't like how it was looking," she combed out my hair again.

Dark gray clouds began to overshadow the morning sunlight. Thunder rolled as the rain outside started to fall.

I frowned. "Man, I hate the rain."

"Really? I love the rain."

I jerked my head. "Why?"

Her hands danced with strands of my hair. "It's cozy to be up against a window watching it fall. It relaxes me. Why don't you like the rain?"

"Bad things happen to me in the rain," I mumbled.

She scoffed. "That's how I feel about snow."

I chuckled. "Snow?"

"Yes. Do not laugh," she said.

I could sense she was pouting.

"Why snow?" I asked.

"Because snow is evil," she proclaimed simply.

"How?"

"It just is," she muttered.

"That's a mess."

"You're a mess."

I felt her hand graze over that one spot on my neck.

I froze.

"Rodrick, how—"

"I got the scar from fighting with my brother," I said quickly.

Her hands softly touched the scar again. "I thought you said that you guys get along."

"Rayden and I used to fight a lot."

"Really? How come?"

I rotated my head toward her slightly. "You're an only child, right? You wouldn't understand."

"That's not true," she stated. "I fight with my cousins, but it's nothing physical."

I furrowed my eyebrows. "That's different; you don't live with them. It's only you, your mom...."

"...And my aunt. I don't have a dad if that is what you are wondering. I mean, I do, but I don't know him," she said.

I wished I didn't know mine. I wanted the world, didn't either.

"My bad."

She continued to braid my hair. "It's okay; I'm a test tube baby."

I choked. "You are what!?"

She laughed. "I'm sorry. I mean, my mom got a sperm donor."

I relaxed again. "She couldn't find anyone? It's not liked your mom is not hot."

"My mom is asexual, Rodrick."

"Really? Why?"

She huffed. "Next time you see her, ask her. As if sexuality is a choice anyway."

"When will that be?" I asked.

She shifted her legs behind me, still playing with my hair. "I don't know when we'll get out of here."

I lay my head on her lap and looked up. I realized that Rahima was the only other girl who I've allowed to touch my hair like this.

"I love your eyes," I blurted out.

I have been surrounded by people with blue eyes all my life, but none compared to hers. Her eyes looked like sapphires and sparkled like them too. Even for an Umbrian, her eyes were striking.

She looked down, meeting my eyes. "I like them too. Now get up so I can finish your hair."

"Why? I'm quite comfy."

Her blue eyes blazed. "Get up."

"I could sleep here."

She moved away.

I secured my arm around her. "Don't kill my fun."

"I'm about to kill *you* if you don't get up."

I moved my arm. "All right, I'm up. No need to be so brash."

"Thank you, Rodrick," she pulled me back and started on my hair again.

And here I thought she was upset.

"I love playing with your hair; it's wavy and such a pretty red. Who did your hair for the meeting?"

"Rona," I answered.

"Really? I didn't know she could do hair."

"She can't; technically, she used diabolism."

She stopped playing with my hair. "She's an Illusionist? I thought she was Human."

I bob my head. "She is on her mom's side. She doesn't use magic around you?"

"No, not at all."

Really? She does it at home all the time. I would have thought she did it outside of the Castle too.

"So, people in Diar are okay with Illusionists?"

"Yeah, you can be anything in our country," I laughed. "That's why so many didn't care that Rona was adopted."

"That's cool. Speaking of your family, why do all your names start with R? Even Rona's?"

I chuckled. "Because both my parents have names starting with R. That is what Riva told me when I asked. And Rona is short for LaRona, so her name doesn't really start with an R."

"Do all of you call your mom by her first name?" she questioned, finishing the end of my hair.

"That is a long story I rather not get into."

I do not like talking about my family.

Do not get me wrong, and I usually butt heads with all of them. Then again, I love each one of them. Even Riva, at times, was rare. I don't know if it's protective or my pride, but I don't talk about my family, and none of them talk about me.

We keep our problems in the family.

"Hmm. I'm done," she finally moved her hands from my head.

I touched my hair; it was in two big braids.

"I hope they look as nice as they feel."

She gave me a dry laugh. "They do; sorry for being nosey about your family."

"Don't be sorry, Arcelia; you didn't do anything wrong."

She wrapped her arms around me. She smelled of fresh lilacs. I gripped her arm. The hug surprised me. I did not know what it was for, yet I wasn't going to stop it.

"I know, Rodrick, but..." she trailed off.

I relaxed more in her arms.

Thunder sounded throughout the room, and lights of lightning shot through the sky. She set her chin on my head, and I laid my head back on her chest, gripping her tighter. We sat together in blissful silence.

For some strange reason, I knew we both needed this.

"Thanks," I said.

She hugged me tighter. "You're welcome."

We had barely known each other for more than a few days, but I felt so at ease with her.

I wasn't really a touchy person off the bat, but with Arcelia, it was different. I didn't mind her touches. And I didn't know why. She was strange yet comforting. She reminded me of home. Not the one back in Diar, but something different. A home I have never had, but I wanted, desperately.

Hopefully, I wasn't going to lose this feeling because it was comforting, nice, new, and refreshing.

Everything about Arcelia seemed that way.

CHAPTER TEN

NIGHTTIME TALKS

I woke up. I twisted toward the bedside clock. "*3:30?*"

I groaned. This was the third time tonight I had woken up. Why can't I sleep? I ran my hands through my long red hair and rubbed my eyes. Today, or going by the time, yesterday, was a long day.

The countless meetings, back and forth with Diar government officials about the whole Ryton fiasco and Riva's unwillingness to cooperate with Rahima and me, it felt like a lot was said, but not a lot was done.

I exhaled and reached for my phone. I dialed Alistine's number.

She picked up on the second ring.

"Hello?" her voice sounded strained.

"Hey, babe."

"He dead, Ray?"

I laughed at Alistine's blunt question.

"No, *querida*—"

"You're dying?"

"No."

She paused. "…You're having a drug relapse?"

"*Jeez, Alistine.* NO."

"Why are you calling me at…1:30 in the morning?"

1:30? Oh. I forgot where we lived was two hours behind the Castle's time.

"Sorry, babe. I couldn't sleep."

"So, your idea is to wake *me up* because you can't sleep, Ray?"

At times, it was hard to read her. Her voice rarely had any passion or emotion. Even when it did, it was hard to tell what emotion she was conveying. Sadly, this was not one of those times. I could hear the annoyance in her voice clear as day.

I breathed out. "I know. I'm sorry."

"So, what is Riva doing now that you didn't call me and complain about already?" she asked me.

I chuckled. "Nothing. I keep thinking about her actions today. I have not seen the woman in two years, and I already want to come back home. Nothing about her has changed at all."

"Don't worry about her," she murmured. "you're there for Rona, *meu amour.*"

She was right. I was here for my younger sister, not my mom.

"Rona is so worried about Rodrick."

"So are you," she sighed. "we all are."

She was right again. Even though Rodrick and I did not connect when we were young, I still loved my brother. No matter how big of a pain in the ass he was, I didn't want anything to happen to him. Especially since we never got to make amends for all the things we did and said in the past. I have not seen him in over a year and now with what was going on…by the Gods.

I hope Ryton does not find him.

"He'll be fine," Ali's voice reassured me. "Rodrick is tough."

"I know."

But so is Ryton.

"Also, you should have taken Rosa with you; she's been crying all day."

I scoffed. "Please, she only misses someone carrying her everywhere."

Ali let out a soft laugh. "If you didn't do it, we wouldn't have this problem."

She yawned. "Go and drink something warm and go to bed. I can't stay awake anymore."

I smiled again. "I will. Love you. Bye."

"Love you. Call me later."

With that, she ended the call.

I grumbled and threw off the covers. I got out of bed and staggered to the door. I made my way to the scullery found down the hall from my bedroom. For some reason, the light in the room was on.

As I entered, I found Riva. At that moment, I wished that sleep would hit me like a brick.

She was sitting at the breakfast table, a large glass filled with what seemed to be wine sat in front of her. Her mouth was closed and bleak. Her cobalt eyes looked morose. Her skin appeared rough and frail. The woman before me looked, not like a Queen, but a miserable old woman, but a *drunk,* miserable, old woman.

"I came to drink some soymilk," I said, monotoned.

I walked over to the fridge. I could feel her glassy eyes on my back.

"My dear, aren't you a bit too old to be drinking warm milk?" she slurred.

"No," I got my glass and poured my milk. I quickly ignited a flame from my palm to warm it.

I turned and headed for the door.

"Come sit," she said.

I stopped. Hesitantly, I sat down across from her. She sipped from her glass.

"Why were you not at dinner? Too busy to join your children?" I asked to break the silence.

She scoffed. "I was working to find that man. Like I did not have enough to worry about when it came to Rodrick...Ryton...he killed the leader of the Zona tribe along, along with her daughter and many... others."

She was struggling as she tried to explain everything to me. "More than 300 women. We-we found the bodies earlier today...."

The thing was, Syth, Rah's husband, already gave us a briefing about the tragic events of the Zona Kingdom. Riva knew this; she just was too drunk to remember it.

I shifted in my seat. "You should really put down the glass once in a while."

I drank from my mug. "At this rate, you're going to die earlier than you should."

She gave me a weak laugh. "Your chi-children would love that, would you children not?"

I took another sip from my mug. "Rahima would be a good replacement for the throne."

She took a sip from her glass. "So, so will you. If you stay sober."

That's funny coming from you.

My eyes narrowed. "Rah is the firstborn; the crown goes to her."

"Not, unless I said otherwise...She must have power over herself before she tries to have power, over others."

Look who is talking.

I slid back in my chair. "She is doing better, Riva. At least acknowledge that."

Her blurry eyes stared at mine. "How is your wife?"

"Why do you care?" I snapped.

I knew she was only calling Alistine, my wife, to mock me. By law, our marriage was annulled. All thanks to the Queen herself. She refused to give royal status to a money-hungry *caipira,* as she put it.

"She is watching over my grandchild," she took another sip.

"Grandchildren," I corrected her.

She smacked her lips. "One is mine by, by...blood."

"When she leaves you, only one will be my bio...blood grandchild," she sneered.

Funny coming from the woman who adopted a maid's child first.

I shook my head. "She is not going anywhere, Riva. You are going to have to get used to that."

"You 'married' someone who used to clean my, no, your... floors. That is so, so, so, sad."

I tightened my fingers around my mug.

Do not let her get to you.

"Riva, she has done more for me than you have—"

"What is with you, boys? My sons and maids? Why do you guys like them?"

Her head bobbed. "Is it a fetish?"

I clenched my jaw.

Do not let her get to you.

Do not let her get to you.

Do not let her get to you.

She gave a drunken laugh. "Rodrick liked Rona's mother because she was a mommy. Do you like Alison because she is a mommy for you too?"

I sneered in disgust. "No. And it's *Alistine.* By the Gods, you are dreadful."

She stopped laughing. "I am not. Do not...think that of me."

"How can I not? You are a sad drunk with more problems than you—"

"You're a sad little drug head!" she yelled. "How many pills have you popped today trying to deal with me!?"

I finished the rest of my milk, rose from my chair, and placed the mug in the sink.

"Goodnight, Riva."

"What, are you going to do some drugs or something?"

I did not respond. It seemed like that would be the only choice I had to be able to tolerate her.

I left the room as the sound of her laugh trailed behind me.

As I walked back to my room, Rahima's door opened. "Are you okay?"

I rubbed my temples. "Yes, Riva is just...."

"...being a pain?" she finished.

I breathed out. "What else would she be?"

She squeezed her hands together. "I can go months without having an outburst or an episode. I get around her one time, and all my progress goes out the window."

"It's like she enjoys seeing like that," Rah whispered.

I rubbed my eyes. "It seems every time we come back; it gets worse."

She scoffed. "It has always been this way."

"No. Not when Maia was here," I whispered. "Riva was still a drunk, but at least we had an *actual* mom, even if for a moment."

Rah exhaled. "Let her soul rest in peace."

I crossed my arms, leaning on the wall. "After she died, everything went from bad to worse."

"We got Rona out of it," she pointed out solemnly.

I looked at Rona's room.

Only because her mom was dead, and her father was practically nonexistent.

We stood in silence.

Unbelievably when we were younger, Riva was, well, more of a decent person. When Ryton was around, it's sad to say she showed some compassion; she was somewhat of a mother. Riva would stay up with me and read bedtime stories, then have tea parties with Rahima in the mornings.

Rah was her day, and I was her night. I remember she still drank but never to the extent of what it was now. When Rodrick became a toddler, was when Riva turned for the worst.

I believed why Rah and I were so destructive as we got older because we remembered—or at least I do—the caring person she once was. It was easier to get her attention when we were doing wrong. We wanted that kind and considerate person back, and for years I thought, stupidly, she would come back.

But it never happened.

This was the woman who would give us kisses at night, the woman who taught us to never let one mistake stop us, the woman whom I used to call mother; she was gone. I realized Ryton found one more thing to take away from us.

I shook my head. "I keep thinking that one day Riva will change. At least for Rona's sake. I thought Maia showed her what being a loving mom could mean."

Rah placed her hands on her hips. "People like Riva do not change; they merely become tolerable."

I sighed. "I'm waiting for the moment she becomes tolerable."

We laughed.

"I've missed you so much."

I turned to her. "What?"

"I've missed you, being able to talk to you without you doped up on something."

I groaned. "Now you sound like Riva. I have been clean for *five* years. Give me some credit."

She shook her head. "The one who should be getting credit is Alistine. Without her, you would be dead by now."

I yawned. "Well, you're right about that. I thank her every day. I cannot see my life without her now."

She smiled at me. "I feel the same about Syth; he helps me so much."

"You know," I started. "I just thought of something."

"What?" she asked.

"You and I found our true loves when we were at the lowest points of our lives."

"Yes?"

I grinned. "Rodrick is not on Waeven alone."

She laughed.

"Maybe Lady Fate is working in his favor for once," she looked to her feet. "He deserves some happiness too."

Out of all of us, Rodrick had it the worst. He'd never really had a loving parent. His older siblings treated him like crap for years. He was the main one taking care of Rona, trying to shield her and himself from the chaos the best he could. Not to mention, he was the Acolyte of Time, which took its toll on anyone. From what I recalled, he struggled to control his powers. His body glowed gold and viciously trembled while he physically altered through random time-lapses. His screams could be heard through the halls of the Castle. It was painful to watch and listen. Shamefully, we never brought it up around Rodrick, and he never talked about it either.

Since I got clean and left the Castle, I had not stayed in touch with my Rodrick very well. I chose to stay away, hidden in the woods. Pretending everything was right in my life, being happy. I cannot even remember Rodrick's birthday; let alone the last time we had an actual conversation. Some brother I was.

Rah shook her head. "We are the worst older siblings."

"Yes, but we are better now," I placed my hand on her shoulder. "Rodrick will be too."

"No, thanks to us," she added.

"Rahima, you cannot blame yourself."

"Why not? I'm part of the problem."

"We both were," I corrected her.

"Me more than you. Every time you guys would fight, I would cry or run away. Like the weak person I am."

"Rahima, stop it. We both did wrong on Rodrick's part. We did get better, and he will forgive us one day. Do not start digging yourself into a hole."

A loud thud came from the scullery. We looked at each other, then to the scullery.

I looked at Rah. "Should we check on drunkie?"

A door creaked. We see Rona tiptoe out of her room. She turned and peeked down the hallway. She jumped slightly when she noticed us.

She tiptoed her way to us. "Did Mom make that sound?"

"I guess so. Why are you awake?" I asked.

"I wake up around this time every night to make sure she's okay or if she needs help getting to bed."

My heart sunk.

Rahima hugged her. "Rona...I'm sorry you have to do that."

Rona shook her head as she wiggled out the hug. "No, I'm fine. I am used to it. Rodrick is usually here to help me get her into bed. If not, I just use magic."

"It's okay," I yawned again. "We can help this time."

Rahima softly chuckled. "Someone's sleepy."

"Yeah, I drank a glass of soymilk. It is starting to kick in," I said, rubbing my eyes.

"Okay, well, I can help Rona with," Rahima peered to the scullery. "her. We will leave you to rest."

"You don't need my help?"

Rona shook her head. "Rahima and I got it. Thank you."

She looked at the scullery. "Can we hurry? I don't hear anything from there, and it is making me nervous."

I yawned. "Okay, but you are sure you don't need help?"

"Night, Ray," Rahima started making her way down the hall.

I sighed.

They should be fine without me.

"Goodnight, you two."

CHAPTER ELEVEN

STROLL DOWN MEMORY LANE

I woke up seeing the sunrise from behind the many jungle treetops. I stretched out on the sofa bed. My feet touched the cool floor. The wind from outside softly picked up. I heard the crumpling paper. My ears perked up, and I twisted around. A large paper sat between the branches of the Bract Epistle Tree.

Mom's letter was here.

I walked over to the desk. As I sat down on the chair, I heard a loud squeak. I froze. It was merely Rodrick turning around on the bed. He was facing in my direction.

In the brim of the sun, I could see some of his features. His long hair spilled out across the pillow and his face. His soft lips were sealed together in a faint line. His straight and thick eyebrows were at ease. His lashes laid quiet on his face. Altogether his face appeared delicate and untroubled.

He looked so peaceful.

I pulled my attention back to the letter:

Arcelia,

I am glad to hear that you and Prince Rodrick have made it to Waeven out of harm's way. Queen Riva and Duchess Rona made it back to Diar safely. Queen Riva informed me of herself. I am sorry that I had to throw you into such confusion. We found out the phony guard was telling the truth; the Demon King is back...

I stopped reading.

This cannot be possible.

He had been dead for over 16 years now.

...During his interrogation, the man confessed to being a follower of the Demon King and a member of the Atar...

I could not be reading it right. I let out a shaky breath, continuing to read:

...He claimed that Ryton was planning on rising soon. A day after you two went into hiding, we believe Ryton attacked the Zona Kingdom. He killed over 300 of their women, including their leader Bellona and her heir, Galian. Last night a bomb was planted at our Palace gates. On it was the mark of the Atar.

Queen Riva, Aunt Cal, and I will continue to stay connected to further investigate the incidents and work on counterattacks.

For now, I want you and Prince Rodrick to protect each other and keep hidden. I do not know how long you and Rodrick will be in hiding. What I know is Ryton will do everything in his power to find the prince. Even if that means...

Why did she scratch out a sentence? Hmm, I wondered what she wanted to write and why she couldn't do it.

...Prince Rodrick can acquaint you better than I could if you have any questions about Ryton. The boy knows more than he is letting on. I am sure of it.

I will let you know when you and the prince can leave the bunker. Until then, may the Gods watch over you.

Stay strong, my dear,

Queen Fayola of Northern Qirar

My hands became clammy, my mouth dry, my eyes strained. I could not believe what I had read. *How could this—*

I heard the creaking sound again. My body tensed. Rodrick was awake. His face mirrored mine. Only it appeared more strained and fearful. His breathing was uneven. He coiled and uncoiled his hands gently.

He must have had a bad dream. He gently turned his head to the empty sofa. His eyes roamed the room. He stopped when he spotted me at the desk. I sat in silence. His tense body relaxed. We stared at each other for what was way too long. I found myself opening my mouth to speak.

"Morning, Rodrick," I said in a softened voice.

"Morning."

"Did you sleep well?"

He huffed. "I guess so."

He laid back down, his hands behind his head.

I made no noise.

I did not know what to say. *Surprisingly.*

I balled my fist gradually, realizing I was still holding Mom's letter.

"Did you have a bad dream?" I placed the letter on the desk and made my way to Rodrick.

I can tell him about the letter later.

His eyes followed me to his bedside. Now that I was closer, I could see the beads of sweat running down his face.

"No. I am fine."

I wiped some sweat from his forehead. "You're lying."

"I am fine," his nose scrunched up. "You didn't brush your teeth."

"I just woke up and stopped trying to avoid—"

He placed his hand in front of his mouth and nose.

I rolled my eyes. "I'll go brush my teeth."

"Uh, yeah," he sassed.

I got up. "When I'm done, we have to talk about what is worrying you. Oh, and you have to brush your teeth."

He sucked his teeth.

While I was brushing, Rodrick decided to get his lazy butt up and join me. Once we were both done, after having a short playfight over the sink, we made our way to the sofa. I grabbed a pillow and hugged it to my chest.

"Storytime," I chirped.

Rodrick looked at me. "Storytime?"

"What is bothering you so much?" I asked.

"Why do you care so much?" he snapped.

I reeled back, surprised at his tone.

"Why don't you want to tell me about it?" I snapped back.

I knew it was none of my business, but it was concerning seeing him wake up so…fearful and anxious.

"I asked you first," he mumbled.

I set down the pillow. "No, I asked *you* first, Rodrick."

He breathed out. "I don't want to bother you with my problems."

I moved closer to him. "You won't."

He slumped his shoulders. "Yes, I will."

I smiled softly. "No, you won't. The energy around you before and after we brushed our teeth is so stiff. Something has to be off."

He ran his hands through his hair.

"I've had …weird dreams," he rubbed his hands together. "They're about my Emblem."

I furrowed my eyebrows. "*Emblem?*"

He lifted his right forearm for me to see, showing me the beautiful gold and bronze marking.

"Ah, I keep forgetting you are an Acolyte."

"That's a good thing in my eyes," he mumbled.

I wondered why he thought that.

I moved closer to him. "Can I see it?"

"You looked at my arm yesterday."

"Right, but I didn't take time to study the Emblem. The giant watercolor skull and rose snake tattoo distracted me."

He shook his head, smiling.

"Fine," he held out his arm to me. "look at it as long as you want."

I glanced at him. "You can tell me about your dream while I look."

I could feel him tense up. "I rather not."

I held onto his forearm. "Why not? Are they that bad?"

"You are nosey."

I smiled. "Yes, I am, but that is beside the point."

He ran his left hand through his hair again. "I will talk about it when I am ready to."

I decided to drop the topic. Rodrick seemed like he was not going to budge. It made me wonder; what was so bad about his dream that he didn't want to talk about it?

"Okay, I give up. You'll talk when you are ready," I directed my attention to the Emblem.

It was gorgeous.

As if Rodrick needed anything else on him that looked good.

The Emblem mainly was gold, which made it glow on Rodrick's creamy skin.

"The symbols represent the Apostles?" I looked up, meeting his eyes.

"Yes. They're their doorways. The bigger ones are for the Allos," he said.

"The Allos? They deal with fate and future, right?"

He shook his head. "You are halfway there. There are four Allos: Sandman, Oracle, Fate, and Anamnesis. Anamnesis deals with memories; the rest should be self-explanatory. Each of them has its own sector in Temporis."

"Temporis is Tempus' realm," I said.

"How'd you figure that one out?" he mocked.

I rolled my eyes, tracing my finger around each ring.

"I am surprised you do not know any of this," he said.

"In school, we learn about the Sycophants and the Acolyte of Death."

"Why?" he asked.

"Qirar has a lot of deep-rooted culture focusing on Mors and his Sycophants. Mors also plays a big part in Umbrian culture, history and is the God we worship. Plus, the current Lady Death is from Qirar," I answered.

"I did not know Lulonah is from Qirar."

I stopped tracing circles on his arm. "You know her?"

He rolled his eyes. "Of course, I do. All four of the Acolytes meet each time the seasons change. It is like the A.J.M. but on a greater scale."

I nodded. It was fantastic to hear an Acolyte's experiences firsthand. Though, I could go without Rodrick's eye roll added to it.

I went back to tracing circles. "Are the smaller circles with the squiggly symbols for the Seasons?"

"They are," Rodrick confirmed.

"I know you have met the Condoras," I finally let go of his arm. "have you met any of the Epochs too?"

"I have only met Day and Year."

I bit my lip. "Have you met *him*?"

"Met who?" he questioned.

The words rolled off his tongue so nicely.

His accent was so smooth; too bad his cockiness masked it most of the time.

I reworded my question. "Have you met Tempus?"

He shot me a slight grin. "Yes, she is—"

I cut him off. "Tempus is a female?"

He scratched his head. "Technically speaking, no, but she uses the pronouns and looks like one."

My eyes sparkled.

Here I was talking to someone who met with one of our four Gods; this was amazing.

And Tempus is a woman!

"When did you meet?" I asked giddily.

He noticed my excitement. "You seem excited to hear about this."

I shook my head eagerly. "I am."

"Why?"

I stared in shock. "Are you serious? You have met one of the four Deorumars, and you expect me to be chill with it?"

He slouched. "I have talked to her so many times that it doesn't really phase me. I kind of forget she is a God."

I pouted. "Lucky."

He chuckled.

"Okay, enough questions, time to tell me about Tempus."

"What do you want to know?"

I pressed my lips together. "Did I not just say enough questions?"

He smirked. "That was a question."

I huffed. "Never mind, tell me about the first time you met him—I mean her."

Rodrick breathed. "Sure thing."

ENCOUNTERING TIME

I opened my eyes. The last thing I remembered doing was touching the center of the Emblem. I was in my bathroom when it started to glow.

Where was I?

I sat on an excellent metal surface. I got up. I stood on top of a grand staircase that overlooked a city. Everything looked straight out of a Steampunk movie.

There were buildings made of metallic material with dark gold lining. They had a modern vintage look to them. They all looked like they were tightly packed together. The sky was clear with a vanilla aroma. There was a light breeze that pushed through my hair. It felt free-floating, even with all the buildings that form rows and rows of barriers.

I turned around and faced a pavilion adorned with copper, gold, and bronze walls. The pearly-white doors caught my eye. Something told me to go inside.

I walked cautiously toward the doors. I stared at them for a moment and touched the engravings of the door. They were wide and rigged and created astonishing branch patterns throughout them. I reached for a door handle, and I tugged it open. I walked into a vast hallway. The walls were decorated with ivory and many pictures of the day, night, and seasons.

I stopped walking. "Where do I go from here?"

I heard light footsteps. They were not of a person but of a hoofed animal. A small female deer came down the hallway on my right side. She was peach in color, with a cluster of bronze spots on her back.

"Hey there," I reached out my hand to pet her. "Do you know where I'm supposed to go?"

Her ears and head perked up. She turned around and began to walk in the opposite direction. She glanced back at me.

"Guess I'm supposed to follow you."

She made a slight sound and turned back around. I followed the small deer down the hallway. We turned a few corners until she stopped in front of a large chiffon door. She glanced at me, then the door.

I looked down at the deer. Her head shifted to the door again.

I snorted. "Guess this is where I am wanted. Thanks."

I petted her head and said, thank you. I pushed the door handle open.

On the other side was a throne room. The throne was a deep bronze color with a dark velvet headrest. It sat atop a five-stepped platform. Behind it was two tapestries, one of the suns setting and one of the moons were rising. There were about eight high arched windows on each side of the room.

Centered on both sides of the throne chair were about ten bejeweled chairs. The ceiling had two massive chandeliers hanging from it. The rest of the room was decked with pretty orange and red decor. Lastly, there was a door on the far left.

As I walked further into the room, the side door opened, and a woman walked through. The lady had a shapely figure and was tall, about seven feet. Her complexion was a glossy brown. Her reddish-purple hair flowed halfway down her back. Her lips, cheeks, and face were all smooth in structure. Her left arm was made of bronze mechanical parts with gold wires that ran through it. Where her heart should be was a giant mechanical clock device. She wore a long champagne skirt that gathered at the bottom. Her left leg peeked through a high slit.

Her top was a bronzed metal corset with a sheer white blouse over it. On her feet were gold-heeled sandals. From what it looked like; she was an important person. And by the looks of that arm, a powerful one too.

She gazed down at me. Her golden eyes met mine.

She smiled. "Hello, Rodrick. I am Tempus."

I raised my eyebrows. *Whoa. This is Tempus? He was a girl?*

"You're a girl?"

She chuckled. "I have no female or male organs. I purely project a form of what a woman resembles on your planet."

She walked over to me. "It is nice to finally meet you."

Tempus extended her long right arm to me.

I timidly shook it.

It felt like a 100-pound weight had been placed in my hand.

Tempus retracted her hand and rotated around, walking to the door. "Please come with me."

"Wait," I said.

She stopped and peered over her shoulder. "Yes?"

"How did I get here? Where is here? Why am I...."

I stopped. *Should I be talking to a God like this?*

"I'm sorry, ma'am," I quickly apologized. "I mean, Goddess."

Her face softened. "It's fine. You are in my dimension, Taporis. I brought you here from your Emblem. I felt now was the best time to finally meet you."

"Oh," I said. Now everything that had happened so far had started to sink in.

"Before you ask me any more questions," she spun back around. "I need you to follow me."

"All right," I said. "Where are we going?"

She pointed. "Through that door."

I went ahead and followed her.

We entered through the door. On the inside, the walls were yellow to purple ombre. It was a room filled with millions of pedestals. Each one had a fancy-looking torsion clock on it. I looked at the torsion clocks. No clock had the same design. Some were rose gold, and some were copper. Some had blue accents; some had silver ones. Some were big, and some were small. Each held its unique beauty. But what was strange was that none of the clocks made a sound.

"This is the Conduct Room. Each of these clocks is a person's individual timeline on Earth," Tempus spoke.

I looked around. "Are there really that many clocks in here?"

"Yes. About 7.9 billion. Each one is in order by birthday and name, birthday coming first."

"Could I see mine?"

Tempus clapped her hands. A few seconds later, a pedestal made its way before us. I thanked her and ran over to it. I touched the glass of the clock and studied how it worked. I furrowed my eyebrows. My watch seemed to be broken.

"Tempus, why is the clock's hand pointing towards 2 but reads 11? And why is the rest of it blank?" I asked.

She came and stood beside me. "Because you are no older than 11 years and 8 months. The hour hands stand for representing your lifeline. When it truly stops moving, it means you have died. When you have made it through another birthday, the number will be added."

She bent down to my height. "If you look closely, you can see how many hours, minutes, and seconds you have been alive."

I tilted my head, peered into the glass dome, and realized she was right. Slowly but surely, the hands moved. I breathed out; I was glad my clock was working.

"What happens if a clock is knocked off from its pillar?"

"Nothing, they are indestructible. Even if you die."

I stood up straight. "Then should you not have more than 8 billion clocks?"

She shook her head. "No, as soon as you pass, everything within the glass dome dissolves into white sand. The sand is given to the Acolyte of Life; they use it to make miracle arrows for dying. The empty torsion clock is transported into another room that I call the Time Pillars. The Time Pillars act as the archives for *all* intellectual beings for established universes."

"Wow. That is awesome. A bit confusing, but awesome," I spoke honestly.

She laughed. "Come now, child. We have done what is needed here. I wanted to show you this room, for it will be more useful in the future. It is time to exit. There will be other times where I will explain more to you in detail."

I nodded my head as I followed her out.

We exited the room, entering the throne room again.

Tempus looked at me. "Rodrick, do you know what you are?"

"I am three-fourths Drakonian and one-fourth Human," I responded.

She gave me a stern look. "Yes, but do you know what your Emblem represents?"

I looked down at my arm where the golden light shined. "No. Not really."

She hummed. "Today, you will find out. Let us go somewhere more comfortable to talk."

I looked around the throne room. "It is so empty. Are you the only one who lives in Taporis besides the deer?"

She shook her head. "Of course not. I have many of my other children living on Temporis."

"So, am I a child too?"

She nodded. "Yes."

"Why don't I live here?" I asked.

"You are too weak to live here. Your body would not be able to sustain in this dimension for so long."

I bowed my head. I hated that she called me weak. I get called that enough at home.

"Even though you may not fit exactly in the category with them in terms of power," Tempus started. "you are still one of my favorites."

I perked my head up. *I am one of her favorites!?*

I grinned widely. "Am I not everyone's favorite?"

"No."

I gasped. "Hey!"

She gasped too. "Oh, I apologize."

I chuckled at *God* apologizing to me. "It is fine. Tempus, for a God, you're pretty laid back."

She smiled. "There is no need to overstress things. Time does not stop for your stress or problems."

The two of us finally exited the throne room. We walked down two hallways as we passed by more paintings and unique colored deer and owls too. Finally, we reached an open walkway with spiraled stairs. We climbed the stairs onto a rooftop deck. The floor was polished marble. The balcony had various fancy seating areas. It was gated in with an overlook of Tempus' vast kingdom.

"This is beautiful," I followed her to a table with two chairs.

"Yes, it is. Now, come sit." I sat down on the soft, cushioned chair. "It is an hour past noon. Are you hungry?" Tempus asked me.

I scratched my head. "Kind of."

Her eyes glowed a bright white. "*Eomc Evaers Em.*"

A giant bird's shadow flew over us. I looked up to see a vast barn owl. He flapped his wings slowly as he landed next to us. He was about four times twice my size.

"Rodrick, what would you like to eat?" Tempus asked.

I messed with the hem of my shirt. "Something with chicken and dessert...like chocolate. Please."

She turned to the owl. "You heard what he wants, quickly."

The owl sounded off and began to fly away.

"Now, while we wait for your food, let us talk about your Emblem."

I looked from Tempus to my arm. "Okay."

"That mark means you are a child of Tempus, a subordinate of mine, my Acolyte."

I squinted my eyes. "I know that part."

She sighed. "Good. You are a vessel, Rodrick. Your job is to be my key and the doorway to and from Taporis and Earth."

"So, I am the only way for you to get to Earth?" I asked curiously.

She nodded. "Yes, as powerful of a God as I am, I still have restrictions."

I laughed. "Why restrict yourself, though? You are a *God*."

"I am not the God who created these restrictions. My sibling Hapesire is to blame. However, these limits help the many universes function without any problems," she spoke.

Her eyes gleamed. "Rodrick, your responsibilities are also to make sure the Seasons on Earth begin at the designated times and make sure the portals to the Allos stay open. Those portals are the connection strings between fate, slumber, memories, and prophecy. They must stay open so the Allos can deliver their gifts to the beings of Earth."

"Yes, I know about connection strings. I have been maintaining them in Diar since I was five."

She must have thought I was just some little kid. I knew what I was doing.

She sighed. "That I know, but Diar is not the only country with connection strings. Every country has it."

My eyes widened. "I am in charge of them too?"

She smiled. "Since you have only been watching Diar's, no one has been regulating the other connection strings. So, they open and close randomly."

"Why are you telling me now?"

Is this why things have been so scary on Earth?

"Rodrick," she sighed deeply. "You were not physically ready to start watching the other portals. I have been doing it in your absence, but as I said, I can only do so much on this side of the playing field."

No wonder the world had been in such bad shape; the Allos play considerable parts in everyone's life. Those connection strings were essential and always needed monitoring. With no connection to them, things on Earth could get chaotic.

Slumber controlled two systems: our bodies and our dreams. The lack of sleep could damage our bodies from the inside out. It could cause us physical harm if we were not in the right mind. Then havoc could wreak on your physical system leading to long-lasting diseases.

Dreams were crucial to emotional and mental health. They played a significant role in providing us with the ability to function. If the connection strings were not open, it could cause night terrors.

Memory did not only hold essential wisdom about our lives but our personality traits as well. It helps us to mentally time travel. The memory could also directly transfer us to past persons that lived through our earlier experiences and see what person or *monster* we were to become.

Fate created luck for both good and bad situations. Our fate was chosen through our actions in the past and present.

Prophecy was vital as it showed control over history, and it predicted what did not happen and what could happen.

With no connection to them, things on Earth could get chaotic.

"I also brought you here to tell you about the future."

I looked at Tempus, confused. "What do you mean?"

She went silent for a bit.

Finally, she began. "Life for you will get much harder. It will take years but trust me; it will be a fate worth waiting for."

She took my hands into her own. "No one has a set future, but eight years from now on this day, you—"

She was cut off by the cry of the giant owl.

Her golden eyes looked to the sky, then to me. "It seems those words were not meant to be spoken."

"What do you mean, Tempus?"

"We can talk more after you eat," she gave me a small wink as the owl carried my food closer.

She never told me what was so important about that day.

MORE HISTORY LESSONS

"...And that is the first time I met Tempus. I apologize if I drew that out. I'm not the best storyteller," he said.

I smiled. "It was a delightful story Rodrick, but next time you go to see Tempus take me with you."

He shook his head. "I can't do that, only I can go to Taporis."

Rodrick gave a dry laugh. "You know, I have thought of running away and staying there, but knowing what can happen here if I do...," his voice trailed off.

His whole demeanor saddened me, something I did not want to see.

"Rodrick, my mom's letter came back. She wrote a lot about Ryton, and it confused me. Can you tell me about him?" I requested in a soft voice. Hopefully, if I changed the subject, it would take his mind off whatever made him sad.

He sighed. "I can."

I fiddled with my thumbs. "Are you going to start or..."

"You asked if I could tell you about Ryton. I said I could, not that I would."

I frowned. "Rodrick, I am serious. Please tell me about him. Why would he be after you? Heck, why are we even talking about him? He died over a year ago."

He laid back on some pillows, exhaling. "Is my sister, okay?"

"Yes, so is Queen Riva."

Even though you did not ask.

He stayed quiet.

I huffed. "Rodrick, we are going to be here for who knows how long. All we can do is sit here and talk to each other. What are you afraid of telling me?"

He bit his lip. "Nothing."

"It has to be something if you don't want to tell me."

He blew air through his nose. "Alright, I'll tell you, but no one else can know. Riva will not play nice if she finds out I ran my mouth."

"I understand; nothing leaves these four walls."

"Not even your mom can know."

I looked him in the eye. "Not even her."

He sat up, took a deep breath, and began. "When Ryton was younger, he found the Abelos."

The Abelos. Everyone had heard of that book. It was what made Ryton become someone of international fame. He had discovered the oldest known encyclopedia on Tempus and her Apostles. Some people say it was written by one of the first Acolytes of Time.

Rodrick continued. "Ryton read about how Tempus could somehow grant wishes to first true followers."

I interrupted. "Do you know who the first followers are?"

He shrugged. "Uh, not really. If I am not mistaken, they are old indigenous tribes. The book said through the Acolyte of Time, and this artifact called the Crest of Time; Tempus would grant his desire."

I stared at him. What was he talking about?

Rodrick seemed to have read my mind. "I know they did not tell you about this in school or anything, but it is the real reason behind Ryton's attacks. The real reason he made the Atar. He is trying to collect all the pieces to the artifact, but they were scattered worldwide and mostly held in museums, temples, and institutions. When he gets all the pieces, all he will need—"

"—Is you," I finished.

He nodded.

I closed my eyes and breathed. "So, is your family the only people who know about this timepiece artifact?"

He shook his head. "No, most of the world leaders also knew. They decided to keep it under wraps, so no one could continue Ryton's philosophy. The Atar never went away, and it just went underground."

Rodrick fiddled with his hair. "The world leaders played Ryton simply to be a man hungry for power and world domination. That is not true. Ryton, unbelievably, wanted uniformity. He wanted a utopian society. A place where we all live under one ruler, law, and social stature. He wanted to go back in time and mold the world into what he wanted it to be."

I cleared my throat. "Why didn't Queen Riva does not follow through with Ryton's plan?"

"At first, she did until she unveiled what that stupid book was about, the creation of a doomsday. She claimed she let Ryton consume her 'better judgment,' she was just another oblivious follower wanting 'peace and equality," he ended with an eye roll.

Every time he spoke of her, it never sat well with me. I felt that he and his mom's relationship was something he would not talk about; so, I did not call attention.

"Okay, I understand all of that now."

I paused, thinking of my following words. "What is his reason for trying to kill you? Would he not need you alive for this to work? Does the mark of Tempus not get transferred to the child who is born when you die?"

He shook his head. "He never intended to kill me. Ryton will not kill me since he needs me so much."

I furrowed my eyebrows. It was the whole reason for putting Ryton in prison. That is what we—I was told.

"It was the easiest way to find him guilty and put him in prison. Riva needed to have a solid reason to place Ryton in prison on Artica, without having to fight tooth and nail with Atar high ranking members, some that happened to be rulers of other powerful countries."

He let out a shaky breath. "Riva and some other leaders could not charge him on international crimes since some of the world leaders were suspected members of his group. So, investigating the matter would take too long. And up until then, most of the world was on Ryton's side."

He sighed. "The world had come out of two decades of wars, merely to be convinced by one man that war was the way for them to live peaceful and happy lives."

I bit my tongue.

"Before I came to the meeting, Riva talked to me about sightings of Ryton. He never died, Arcelia."

I gasped, covering my mouth. I didn't know what to say.

Rodrick patiently waited for me to get my thoughts together.

"I am with you," I said. "you can continue."

"I know that soon I will have to leave—"

"What!?" I exclaimed. "You can't leave!"

He looked at me with sad eyes. "He is going to find us eventually. I can feel it. I don't know exactly how it works, but I think that if he gets a certain number of pieces, my arm becomes a beacon."

He paused.

"He doesn't care how many lives he takes. If he gets what he wants, that's all that matters."

I sat up. "I'm already in this thing with you. There is no turning back now."

Rodrick groaned. "I don't want you getting hurt because of this, because of me."

"I won't," I said.

"You will," he snapped.

We sat in silence.

"Arcelia?"

His voice sent a chill down my spine. "Yes?"

"You know what I was taught to do when I was younger?"

I tried to playfully roll my eyes. "Of course, I don't know."

He ran his fingers through his hair. "I was told that when Ryton would come back, that I am to take him out."

I gulped. "They want you to kill Ryton?"

"Yes, and I will."

I shook my head. "Rodrick, you—"

He cut me off. "Have other options? Like what? If he's put in jail, he'll find a way out. If I stay on the run forever, he will kill everyone in his path until he finds me. What, you want me to 'talk' him out of it?"

I looked down at my feet.

He was right. Rude about it, but right. There was nothing else he could do. I mean, killing one man who has killed hundreds of others would be justified.

Right?

"I am sorry," I mumbled. "I don't know a lot about this. You've had years to think about it; I've had minutes."

He shifted closer. "I didn't mean to snap at you. You've done nothing to be sorry about on my part."

I felt the sting of tears in my eyes. Rodrick wrapped his arm around my body, pulling me to his chest.

"Why are you tearing up?"

I gave a dry laugh. "Honestly, I don't know."

Was I scared? Angry? Worried?

I had no clue. All I knew was Rodrick was with me, and I felt secure that when he was. Better he is here with me than anywhere else with the Demon King.

I sighed. "Thank you for telling me everything."

He hugged me tighter. "You're welcome."

CHAPTER TWELVE

Room for One Guest

"I want you all out of the country by tomorrow morning," Mom said calmly.

Ray eyed her. "All of us?"

"Yes, including your *family*," she drained her large glass of red wine. "All your arrangements have been made for when and where you are to go."

No one uttered a word.

"I think I should leave with Syth," Rahima said, disrupting the silence.

Her voice was low, and she made no eye contact.

"Why? You need your husband to babysit you?" Mom asked.

Rahima bit down on her lip, tapping her finger on the surface of the table.

"Leave Rah alone, Riva," Ray called out in her defense.

"Rayden, honestly, I do not know why she came. Her husband is the one in the military and the only person right now trying to actively help me with this whole Ryton fiasco."

"First, that's a lie. And second, you wanted us here for Rona's sake," Ray spat back.

"She only needed one sibling to come."

"I'll leave today," Rahima's voice was barely above a whisper.

"Always the first to run," Mom said.

Rah gripped the table.

"Leave her alone, Riva," Ray warned.

Riva raised an eyebrow. "When did you become my daughter's mouthpiece."

"Oh. So now I'm your daughter?" Rahima snapped.

"What are you blabbing about? You have always been my daughter—"

Rah's claws dug into the wooden table. "Really!? Because half the time, it seems like the only daughter you want is Rona!"

"Rah, calm down," Rayden glanced at Mom. "She's not worth losing your breath over."

"And Alistine is?"

Ray balled up his fist. "Riva. *Calar a boca.*"

Mom stayed stone-faced. "If I choose not to? What? Will you or your sister do?"

"Mom," I pleaded. "please leave them—"

"Rona stays quiet; adults are talking," her hand gripped her empty glass.

As much as I wanted to say something, I did not.

"Do not talk down to her!" Rahima's claws cracked the smooth surface of the table.

"Don't break the furniture. By the Gods, you act like some savage."

Rahima lost it. She kicked back her chair and charged at Mom. Ray quickly caught her and pushed her away toward the wall.

"Let me go, Ray!" She screamed as tears ran down her face. "One good slap is all she—"

"Where did I go wrong with you?" Mom shook her head in disappointment.

Ray whipped his head toward Mom, furious. "Get. Out."

"This is my—"

"Mom, please leave," I cut in. "Ray, I'm going to get Syth," I brushed quickly past Mom without another word.

Some of the servants had started crowding around the door. I told them to go away as I rushed to find Syth. Even down the hall, Rahima's screams could be heard. Yup, this is how I wanted to spend time with my family.

Just lovely.

TIME TO TALK

Rona was able to get Syth, and thankfully he was able to calm down his wife.

Rahima decided to go upstairs and start packing to leave Diar. After Rah made her way to her room, I joined Riva in the dining room again.

A servant was pouring what I think was vodka into Riva's glass. The two of us had been sitting in silence for about ten minutes.

The only sound came from Rona when she made her way back into the room.

"Why do you always do this?" I questioned.

Riva straightened herself in her chair. "What do you mean, Rayden?"

"He means, why do you always try to make Rahima snap?" Ro finished for me.

Riva sipped her drink. "The way I speak to her is no different from the way I speak to you."

I placed my hands on the table. "You're right, it's not, but just because words don't hurt physically doesn't make it fine to say hurtful things to your children."

"You stopped being children even before seventeen. You always have—"

"I know how we have always been. Even before Ryton left. I know that I was better off when he was around. It seemed like you had someone to keep you in check," I said.

"Rayden, you are no one to speak. At times you were worse than he was. So, keep your mouth shut," her eyes shifted to her glass as she clanked it down on the table.

I stood up. I was not sitting through this crap again because I knew Rona could not hold me back.

"Stop acting like a God above us, Riva. You're worse than me, my siblings, and Ryton combined."

Riva knew she had a drinking problem.

Before I was born, she had it after I was born when I was on drugs, and now after I'm clean. Yet, it doesn't bother her in the slightest to stop. Even when she knows it's the reason, she is so destructive and damaging.

"May I please be excused?" Rona asked.

I relaxed.

I hated fighting in front of her. She did not deserve to see us like this. Nevertheless, she always did.

"Yes, dear, you may," Riva spoke gently.

Even Riva looked slightly uncomfortable with Rona here.

"Thank you," Rona quickly got up and spoke a spell. "*Diaear.*"

She vanished.

I scowled at Riva. "Listen here, your old bat, keep trying my patience; you know what I can do when I'm angry. So, for your sake, don't talk to me until I leave this miserable place."

I turned to exit.

Riva said, did nothing as I walked out, but I could feel her eyes on me as I left.

After Syth had taken Rah upstairs to her room, she tried to get some sleep. But trying to be a good brother, I had to make sure she was ok. Now I was sitting on Rah's ottoman in her room with her next to me. She was dressed in fluffy pajamas and her hair in a messy ponytail.

"Okay, Rah, what do you want to fume about?" I asked.

Over the years, Rah and I had always been close, even when I was an addict.

She always looked out for me. I knew her well enough to know that when she had an outburst, she needed time afterward to rant about why she had the outburst in the first place.

She let out a heavy sigh. "Why does she feel she has the right to bully us, then act like she has her crap together? I mean, if you call being a depressed drunk having your stuff together, she would be the queen of that too!"

I sat still and listened.

"She acts like she's better than us, and that's the only reason she needs to set her expectations so high!"

She formed a fist. "Maybe she should have put us in prison with Ryton!"

I saw the tears start to form in her eyes.

"Why does she think it's okay for her to treat her kids like trash?"

The tears flowed down her face. "Why do I have to act like everything is okay? I take my medicine every day, and still, I'm barely straight in my head."

She dragged her claws across the ottoman. "I have to lie to Rona and you and Syth and pretend like I'm getting better. Then there's Cecil...I'm too scared to even bring him around the rest of this family."

Her breathing started to become ragged. I wrapped my arms around my sister. I pulled her to her feet and guided her to the bed.

She continued to sob.

I hugged her even tighter. "You're okay, you're okay."

After about ten minutes of her endless crying, she began to calm down.

"Sorry for covering your shirt with tears and snot."

"I have little kids running around everywhere, so I am used to it," I laughed.

"Ray, thank you."

I gently pulled away. "All I did was hug you."

She shook her head. "For some people, that's all it takes, even when it comes to people like Riva."

I sucked my teeth. "People like her need more than a hug."

"Yes, maybe," she looked down at her feet. "her depression is getting worse."

My face dropped. "I was able to find the help I needed thanks to Ali, but more so more my physical health over my mind. I am scared that for her to find help, Ryton must go. Permanently and never come back."

She slumped her shoulders. "Even though that thing killed all those innocent people, she was much better when he was around."

She shook her head. "We are supposed to be trying to piece together a way to stop Ryton and protect Rodrick. But no, we're too busy bickering."

A light knock turned our attention to the door.

"You can come in, Syth."

The door opened. A tall, blond man with a bionic arm stood in the door frame. He was wearing a short-sleeved military uniform. His arm gleamed in the sunlight.

"How did you know it was me, *belo*? Hello, Rayden."

"Hello, Sy," I saluted.

Rah beamed at her husband. "Honey, you're the only person who knocks besides my brothers and the servants. And you greet people before you ask questions."

"Ah, yes. I apologize, my love," The cyborg answered.

"You are fine," she smiled.

Shouldn't he apologize to me too?

Syth entered the room.

"Did you polish your arm?" I wondered, squinting my eyes, as I found it hard to see him entirely in the light.

He nodded stiffly. "I apologize if the reflected light bothers your eyes."

Rah got up and wrapped her hands around his neck. "You're fine, my love."

I rolled my eyes. I was the one who was bothered by it, not her.

His hazel eyes watched her closely. "Are you fine?"

She smiled. "Yes."

He wrapped his arms around her waist.

This is my queue to leave.

I got up from my seat. "Let me go before you make a sibling for Cecil."

Syth was mystified. "Why would you think we are trying to reproduce?"

"Get out, Ray," Rahima spoke over Sy.

I chuckled. "I'm leaving. I was playing Syth."

"So, it was a joke?"

"Yes."

His face became even more perplexed. "But it was not funny."

Rah threw her head back in laughter. "Sweetie, I love you."

He smiled. "I know, *eu te amo.*"

I scoffed playfully as I made my way now to Rona's room. Sy always seemed to keep Rah's spirits and emotions in balance. While Rah seems to restore Syth's humanity in the littlest ways. They both had come so far. Hopefully, the rest of us can do the same.

Dinner to Ourselves

I breathed out and glimpsed at the grand clock in the hallway. It read 5:30—one more hour before he comes.

I gazed out the stained-glass windows. Through them, the sun was setting. My plan to get Rayden, Rahima, and Rona out of the country today went smoothly.

Even though their visit ended on a sour note. Which all of them usually do. It didn't matter. My kids were out of harm's way.

Not bad for some "drunk old hag."

Contrary to popular belief, I am not a drunk; instead, merely a woman who prefers wine over regular grape juice.

Everyone had a way to numb her or his pain. Even Rayden, who stopped using drugs, turned around and now smokes cigarettes. Even though he said he only smokes when stressed. Which baffled me on what he could be worried about. I run one of the most influential and wealthiest countries on our side of this solar system. And he claimed he is stressed? Please.

I keep most of my family's business out of the eyes and ears of the public. I worked my way to the top of the food chain and have stayed there for years. I pulled Diar from the hated ashes left by Ryton. I reclaimed the beauty that was Diar again, all by myself.

Yet people still think so lowly of me, especially my children.

Even if they did not realize it, I loved them. They were the reason I left Ryton. They were the reason I turned on him.

Ryton was my world for so long.

He was the only thing that mattered. Then the Gods blessed me with Rahima and Rayden. I thought that the world Ryton was molding would be safer for them. Then Rodrick was born, and everything changed. My last baby boy and the new Time Acolyte. My true gift from the God Tempus themselves.

He was beautiful, and I was selfish. How could I give him over to Ryton? I couldn't, and I wouldn't. Not then and not now. At least, not without a fight.

I may have worshiped Ryton, but my love for my children was greater.

Even Rona, who was not my child by birth, had an I piece of my heart. The Gods delivered me, Rona, in exchange for the child I did lose, and she meant so much to me. I would give my life for any of them in a heartbeat. If they knew the things, I would do for them, they would be more thankful. They were the only reason I fought to stay queen of a country that hated me so much. They were the reason I stayed with a man who never loved me. They were the reason I was able to bear each day.

I regret nothing I've done for my children but will forever regret everything I didn't do.

But even as much as I loved them, the hold Ryton had on me still proved to be more significant. No matter how much I tried to fight it, to combat it, all I could simply do was run away. It always seemed to work out better for me that way. I regret nothing I've done for my children but will forever regret everything I didn't do.

The sound of familiar footsteps snapped me out of my thoughts.

"How was the press meeting?" I asked.

"Uneventful, my queen," Syth said. "Though, I believe you should have been there."

I shook my head at my son-in-law. "It would have made no difference."

"That we will never know."

He finally made his way over to me and gave me a bow. "Your *Highness*."

I rolled my eyes. "If I want someone to mock my title, I would have kept my children here."

He shook his head. "They are not children. Rona at thirteen has more sense than some officials in your military."

"There's a reason you came to speak with me, Syth. What is it?" I folded my arms.

He was silent for a moment. "You know he will come alone?"

I studied the cybernetic man. "Is that a question or a statement?"

"It depends on how you are willing to answer it."

I glared at him.

"It was a question."

I groaned. "Syth, stop it."

His brown eyes stared at me in confusion. "Stop what?"

I rubbed my temples. "Nothing."

My eyes trailed to his left metallic hand; his uniform jacket covered the rest of it.

"If you will not give me the real reason why you are here, I will use this time to my own accord."

"How so?" he asked.

"I want you to be one of the escort guards for tonight's dinner," I said.

"Why? Will me being there advance this theory of yours?"

I narrowed my eyes. "What theory?"

"That Ryton must die, at least *genuinely* this time."

I gestured to his artificial limb. "Do you shoot well with that arm?"

"Yes."

He lifted his arm as if it were a flawed prize. "Yet, I will not be shooting at anything tonight."

"Why is that?" I refolded my arms.

"For one, it would not make a difference," he walked over to peer out of the stained-glass windows. "and two, I was not born into this family, Riva."

I pressed my lips together. "I am aware that you married Rahima."

He turned his body fully to me. "Correct, I was *married* into this family. This is a family matter."

I narrowed my eyes. "So, because of that, you will not kill Ryton?"

"I cannot kill Ryton. No matter how well I aim at him or how close I am. I cannot be the one to kill him today."

I stood there, speechless.

He sounded foolish.

Who does he want to kill Ryton?

He continued. "If you could do it, you would have done it years ago. You have too close to a bond. Rona cannot be the one either. She and I are in the same boat."

I stayed quiet. I knew whom he was trying to get at, but I let him continue his stupid justification.

"Maybe Rayden, though he may be in the same predicament as you. Rahima's mental state would crumble against him."

"Rodrick cannot—"

"Why not?" he asked. "You made sure he was trained to do it. He is the whole reason for this."

I know what I did, but there was no proper way to prepare for Ryton.

I shook my head. "I've already done enough damage concerning my son."

"Rodrick has to kill him," Syth said. "I know you had already thought about it, even before we started this conversation."

"Syth," I said in a warning tone.

The sun hit his silver neck implants, blinding me for a moment. "I am sorry, Queen Riva. I care for Rodrick like everyone else in this family, but—"

"How can he kill someone when he is not present?" I retorted.

"Who said Ryton is going to die today?"

I gritted my teeth. "Enough, Syth. If Ryton comes here and he does not comply with my demands to stop all this madness, then I'll end him myself."

He scoffed. "Riva, I may be oblivious at times, but I am not stupid. You and I both know you will not do that. If you could, we would not be here right now."

The dinner was in three minutes. I sat patiently in the downstairs dining room. A servant came in.

"My Queen," he bowed. "Your guest has arrived."

I got up and straightened my clothing. I was wearing a long teal dress with gold and white embroidery. My hair was pinned up under my crown.

"Let him in and make sure all the doors are locked once he is inside," I looked at him pointedly. "including this one."

"Yes, my Queen," he bowed and left.

I carefully circled the table.

Everything was in its place. The chandelier shone brightly in the room. The hutch was dusted off and polished.

There were two plates set on either side of the dining table. Steam and the aroma from the food filled the room.

My reflection gleamed on the hard, dark wood. The centerpiece was a beautiful display of wild poppy flowers. Pinks and greens brimmed from each of their petals. Everything was perfect. The plates, the silverware, the drinks—the drinks. *Did he still drink?*

I reminisced about the times when we would lavish ourselves with bottles of pure white wine. I hated white wine, but I drank it because he liked it. He would always pour my glass halfway. I would try to convince him to finish the job, and he would tease me about being such a lightweight. We would go back and forth about it until we ended up fighting over the bottle, spilling it everywhere.

We were happy.

I was happy.

I messed with the ring on my finger. I decided to wear a wedding band. It sparkled in the light. It felt light on my finger but heavy on my heart.

The door opened. I turned.

A guard and a man were standing in the door's entryway. The guard bowed to me and left, closing the door behind her. I heard the door lock.

He wore an oversized wool jacket and dark circular sunglasses, and his hair was hidden underneath a black hat.

We stood there together, alone. The guest took off his hat and placed it on the table, revealing his dark gray and crimson hair. His hair was groomed with a rippled quality.

His cheekbones had begun to sink. His skin was tan and brushed with wrinkles. Still, he was the same beautiful man from all those years ago. He walked over to me.

"Ryton," I whispered.

He stopped in front of me. "Riva, *minha beleza*."

I removed the glasses from his face. His entrancing green eyes shined. He stroked his hand through my hair, lifting my chin. Our lips joined.

"I have missed you," he said as we pulled apart.

I couldn't tell if he was lying or not. "Shall we eat?"

We sat on opposite ends of the table. He cut through the steak on his plate.

"It's rare. I am surprised you remembered."

"How could I forget?" I said as I took a bite of my steak.

How could I forget anything about you?

We sat peacefully for the rest of our meal.

"This is nice," he sipped on his glass of white wine.

"Thank you. It is my personal favorite," I said, glancing at him.

It was a lie.

I only ever drank white wine when I was around him. That is why I have such a love for red wine now since Ryton hated it so much.

"I can tell. I could taste it on you when we kissed."

I stiffened; that was a lie too. He knew I was lying, and that was never a good thing for me.

I pressed my lips together. "I did not drink before you came."

"Riva, I'm not a fool," he began. "You hate white wine. You always have. It is a shame that you are still trying to kiss my feet after sixteen years."

I narrowed my eyes. "I—"

"Don't try and deny it, Riva. I see through you as easily as I see through this glass," he said.

I put my fork down.

"You still seem so self-centered after all this time." I shot back.

He scowled. "You have three children and still only care for yourself. Then say—"

I raised my head. "I have four children."

"You never got pregnant after the boy."

"Ryton—"

"You killed my last child then replaced her with some peasant's."

"I had a miscarriage."

He banged his glass on the table.

I closed my mouth.

"Do not try me, Riva. I am no fool."

Relax, I told myself, *relax.*

I looked him in the eye. "You did not come all this way to talk about the past."

His eyes hardened. "You're right; I did not."

He withdrew his claws.

His body moved toward me as his claws lightly scraped the table. "You know why I am here."

I rose from my seat. "Rodrick is not here."

"I know," he stopped in front of me. "I want to know where you hid him. And I want my Crest pieces."

"You thought that I would just tell you? You came all this way for nothing," I scowled.

He smirked. "I also came to see you, *meu amor.*"

"I do have some idea of where he is; however," he looks down at me. "I'd rather not waste my time trudging through all of Waeven to find him."

I stared at him in shock. *How did he know?*

"What? You think I didn't know?"

He laughed. "I told you, I can see through you like glass. I have eyes on every level of Diar and this Castle. I always know what is going on. *Always.*"

I stayed quiet.

"Still," he lifted my chin with a pointed claw. "I want my queen with me. I have deeply missed you."

He leaned in closer, but I turned my head.

"No, Ryton."

"You know you missed me," he traced his clawed finger over my jaw to my bottom lip. "You were my world, Riva."

Lies. He is lying. I told myself.

I tried to back away from him, but he grabbed my wrist tightly.

I pulled my arm back. "I don't care how much you claim to love me. I won't let you harm my son."

"Is he not my child, too?" he tugged me closer.

I scoffed. "Not for the last sixteen years."

He launched his hand at my neck and pushed me against the wall. The hutch next to me shook with the force of his aggression.

"Queen Riva, is everything alright?" I heard a guard calling from the other side of the door.

Ryton turned his eyes from me to the door back and me.

He released my neck slightly. "Answer him."

"Yes," I said, trying not to sound so shaken. "I am fine. Stay at your post. I simply bumped into the cabinet."

"Yes, my Queen."

It went quiet.

Ryton leaned into my ear. "Good girl."

His grip tightened on my neck as I tried to pry his handoff.

He combed through his hair. "Riva, very soon, the new world I envisioned will become a reality. I just need that boy, those pieces and you."

I scratched at his hand. "You will never succeed."

He chuckled. "Your face is red."

He licked his lips. "You know your blood is my favorite shade of red."

"Ryton…" I struggled to speak.

The room was spinning, and I was getting dizzy. My eyes were blurry from the tears flowing down my face. I sensed something trickle down my throat. I could feel each of his claws threatening to poke holes into my neck.

"Please..."

He let go. "Your act is beginning to get old, Riva. You know I will not kill you."

"W-what act?" I said between ragged breaths.

"You know how to fight. I have seen you fight and bend others to your will so easily. For some reason, you always forget how to fight when—"

"You beat me," I spat out.

He placed his hands in his pockets. "See what I mean? So dramatic. It's called putting you in your place."

He walked back to his side of the table.

"My scars say otherwise."

"What scars?" he scoffed. "You're half Drakonian, you have thick skin. Plus, you always loved to push people's buttons, and you know my temper."

Yes, one thing my kids seem to have gotten from you.

His eyes softened. "I am sorry, *bonita*."

I held my neck; it was tender to the touch, and my skin felt frail.

The air in the room was stiff.

"Riva," he murmured. "It is time for me to leave."

No! I must try to stop him.

He grabbed his things. "I will find the boy. When I do, I'll come to you."

He spoke as he placed his glasses and hat on. "I will take you by force if need to."

"You will not be successful."

Why am I so dizzy?

He sneered. "You joined me once on my quest. It will not be hard for you to do it again."

"Ryton," I could barely draw air to my lungs. My body gradually lost feeling. I slid down to the floor.

"You... put...poison in your claws," my words were slurred.

"Only a small amount, *minha querida*. It'll wear off in a few minutes, I believe. The sad result of you also being part Human."

He moved to the door. "I will come to see you again."

"Yes...with my foot...at your neck," I managed to get out.

He gave a low chuckle. "I believe you left my pieces in the same place in the Castle. It's like you wanted to make this easy for me."

I tried to crawl over to him.

He leered. "You look so hopeless; it is quite refreshing to see."

I have...to...stop him.

Ryton chuckled. "Till next time, my love."

My eyes slowly shut.

CHAPTER THIRTEEN

CAPTIVATION VACATION

"Celia, I need to do something. We need to do something. I'm tired of being here like sitting ducks."

Rodrick paced around the small, cramped room.

He had been complaining about needing to do something other than sleep and count the days going by for a while. He did not want to sit and wait for that demon to come to find us.

I understood where he was coming from, but after reading my mother's letter. What more could we do? Ryton had just killed 300 women; what more to kill the two of us?

"What do you want me to do?" I said, turning to him from my place on the futon.

He stopped pacing, and a grin formed on his lips. "Entertain me?"

"No."

He stretched. "Why not? You didn't even hear what I was going to suggest."

I crossed my arms. "I have a pretty clear idea of what you meant."

"Oh, really?"

"Yes, you *punda*," my eyes grew big at what I'd just said.

Oh my gosh, did I just call him—

He laughed. "I've been called worse."

"I'm sorry. I didn't mean to call you that. I just lost my cool."

He rolled his eyes. "I told you I'd been called worse."

"Really?" I asked.

"Most people think that I am the cause of the whole Ryton thing. You act as if you've never heard any of those stories about me," he said back.

I gave a dry laugh. "You mean how people think you're an arrogant, self-entitled brat?"

"Yeah," he paused. "Do you think that?"

I opened my mouth then closed close it.

Do I?

I mean, overall, Rodrick was a chill guy. He could be very, very arrogant. He had not really come on to me in the last three days. The only real thing he had done was tease and joke. He kept to himself and gave me space, too.

"I mean, you could be?" I looked down at my feet; I didn't want to meet his eyes. "From what I have seen, no."

He walked back around to come to sit next to me.

He relaxed back on the futon. "Good to know someone thinks different of me."

I shrugged. "I guess so."

"Your accent is so cute," he blurted out.

I puffed my cheeks. "No, it's not."

"It is no need to be shy."

"You still bored?" I asked, trying to change the subject.

I hated it when people talked about my accent. Usually, what happened next was pointing out all the wrong ways I pronounced words.

"Yes, I need more of a distraction from the situation we are in."

"So, I'm a good distraction?" I wiggled my eyebrows.

He laughed. "You are, but my mind is still racing."

I crossed my arms.

"What can we do?" I asked, saying it more to myself than anything.

My eyes studied the windows. We could leave, only for a moment, of course.

"Do you want to go outside?" he asked.

I raised my eyebrow. "How do you know I wanted to go outside?"

"I used context clues," he grinned. "You've been glancing at the windows for a while now."

"Oh, really?"

He nodded. "Most of us smart people are excellent at using context clues."

I got off the bed and sat next to him. "Like you're smart, Rodrick."

He shrugged. "I made it into Shrone University."

I looked at him, surprised.

Shrone University was known as one of the best universities on the planet. It did not matter who your parents were, what country you come from, how much money you made, or if you were a member of royalty.

Not just anyone could get into Shrone.

"I wouldn't expect that you would get into such a prestigious university," I spoke truthfully.

"I hear that a lot," he rested his head on my lap. "Believe it or not, I do like to learn, only if what we are learning interests me."

"What do you want to major in?" I asked.

"Transpersonal Psychology."

Whoa.

I stared at him.

He gave me a confident grin. "Not what you were expecting, was it?"

I shook my head. He cracked another smile. This one was different from the others I had seen from him. This one was not out of pride or anything like it. This one was soft and felt genuine. Even though it was a small one, it fit Rodrick's face quite nicely. I liked it.

"Why did you pick that major?" I questioned.

"I want to know how peoples' emotions and spiritual states intertwine and how it justifies their actions," his tone was lax but convincing. "Maybe communicate that knowledge to those who don't understand."

What he was telling me was coming from the heart. I could feel it.

Though I have known Rodrick for a brief time, I would not mind getting to know him more. He was something new and intriguing.

Even when this mess is over, I just can't help but want to know and learn more about who he indeed was.

More of this genuine and honest Rodrick, not the cocky prince everyone portrayed him to be.

Eventually, when this mess is all over. He was something new and intriguing. I just couldn't help but want to know and learn more about who he indeed was.

"Arcelia, you here with me?"

I blinked a couple of times. "Yeah, I got distracted by your voice."

I gave myself a mental slap. *You idiot, why did you say that?*

Rodrick gave a faint chuckle. "I did not know my voice could be so enticing."

Now it was my turn to laugh. "It's not that great."

"It can be. *Minha linda dama,*" he shot back.

I looked away. "No comment."

He laughed again. "You said you were eighteen, right?"

I responded. "Yes. Why do you ask?"

"So, are you in college too, or is it different in Qirar?"

I shook my head. "No, I am taking a year off."

"You don't know what you want to do?"

"How'd you guess?"

He shrugged. "A friend of mine is doing the same."

"You have friends?"

He sucked his teeth. "Yes, I have friends. Why does that surprise you?"

"You look like a person who doesn't have a lot of friends or any friends at all," I said.

He scoffed. "Yeah, I get that a lot too. I have a small group of close friends and too many associates."

I grinned. "I have a small circle too, but most of my friends are my family."

"Really?" I could tell that he was trying not to laugh.

I crossed my arms. "It's not funny; I'm close to my family."

Well, at least with my cousins.

"Yeah..." his voice trailed off.

"Rodrick, are you okay?"

He blinked slowly. "Yes, sorry. I got lost in thought."

I pressed my lips together. "So, are you okay?"

"Yeah."

I played with his hair. "Thinking about someone?"

He shifted in my lap. "What?"

"Is someone on your mind?" I didn't know where I was going with it, but I had an urge to ask.

"Yea, my sisters, and brother, especially Rona. If I'm here worrying about her, I know she is doing the same."

His body tensed up. "I don't like her or anyone to worry about me. I have taken care of myself fine for all these years."

I combed through his locks. "Everyone needs someone to worry for them; it's a way of showing you that they care."

"It's not the only way..." he mumbled.

"Rodrick, have you ever really talked to anyone about this?"

His blue eyes flickered to me. "What do you mean?"

"Do you talk about your family? Like I know this may come off harsh, but you seem to have a lot of problems."

He gave a dry laugh. "I do. I don't have anyone to talk to about my, well, my family's issues. Riva is the queen of Diar, and on top of that, she has custody of Rona. She could take her away from me if I said too much."

He went quiet.

I reached for his hand and squeezed it. "I don't know how long we are going to be here, but while we're here, we could talk about it."

"No," he said. "I don't want to talk to you about my family problems."

"Who will you talk to then?"

He turned his head. "I don't know you."

I smiled softly. "It's easier to talk to a stranger about your problems than someone you know."

For the first time, Rodrick looked...nervous?

"But" he groaned. "Arcelia, you cannot fix anything."

I gently rubbed his arm. "I know. I'm here to listen, for you to vent to."

I intertwined our hands.

"It's a lot," he warned.

"We have time."

He looked down. "I don't know where to start."

"I can tell you some things about my family first. Are you ok with that?"

He let out a breath. "Sure."

"Okay, do you remember when I told you my mom got a sperm donor, and I don't know my dad?"

He rolled his eyes. "How can I forget? Test tube baby."

I giggled, then started start to frown. "It's a lie. She knows my father. I know my father."

I looked at the ceiling. "They dated. When she got pregnant with me, she left him and moved to Qirar with my aunt. He moved on, got married, and had four more kids."

I bit the inside of my cheek. "When I found out about him, I wanted to meet him. So, I tracked him down, called him, and asked him if he would meet with me. He agreed."

Rodrick sat next to me, not saying a word.

I played play with my fingers. "The day his plane was supposed to land in Qirar, it crashed. He was one of the passengers who didn't survive. That was six years ago. I still blame myself for his death. I know that if I didn't try to meet him, he would still be here."

They don't call Umbrians 'Children of Death' for nothing.

I hold my breath, trying my best not to cry. The air in the room was stiff. I'm sure you could have heard a pin drop.

I exhaled. "I know I'm leaving a lot of stuff out, but this isn't about me. Just know Rodrick, no family is perfect and happy, no matter how much power we hold."

He relaxed his shoulders. "Thanks for telling me."

I ran my hands through his hair again. "You're welcome."

"My mom is an alcoholic," he began.

SHED YOUR TEARS

Arcelia looked at me in shock. Her eyes looked like they were about to pop out of their sockets. "She's—what!?"

Dang, I knew I shouldn't have told her. I don't know what came over me. The words just flew out of my mouth.

"I—Rodrick, I'm sorry for my reaction. I was not expecting that. You just threw it out in the air, so…suddenly."

She gives me a weary smile. "You can continue; I'll be quiet."

I laid down next to her, never letting go of her hand. I bit my lip. I'm so nervous. I didn't know what made me more nervous, Arcelia's presence or telling her about my problems.

"Since I was young, Riva has had that *problem*," I started.

She caressed my hand, edging me to go on.

"My older sister and brother said she was better before I was born because Ryton was in the picture."

I ran my hands through my hair. "Every year, her drinking gets worse. When my siblings or I bring it up, Riva gets defensive, and it always causes a fight. I don't know why she drinks, and I don't know if I want to know. I mean, I know she has depression, but..."

I pushed myself deeper into the sofa cushions. "It is so stressful. She is there but not there at the same time. She doesn't deserve the title of 'mom,' at least when it comes to me."

"So, you never had someone there, as a parent in your life?" Arcelia asked me.

I faced her. "I did, Rona's birth mom."

I shifted my eyes to the wall. "Her name was Maia; she was a maid at the Castle. She died a couple of months after Rona was born."

Maia was a mom for my older siblings and me. Nonetheless, she and

I had the closest bond.

Arcelia squeezed my hand harder. "When she died, it was like the tipping point for all of us. All the crap hit the ceiling."

I let out a shaky breath.

"Rodrick, do you need a moment?"

I shook my head. "No, I spaced out for a second."

I looked at her. "I feel stupid for not asking this earlier, but can you not tell anyone about the things we're talking about?"

She bit bites her lip. "As long as you do the same for me."

I looked her in the eye; they were soft and comforting. They made me feel warm and at ease with continuing.

Should I tell her about Ray's problem and Rahima's issues?

No. I can't.

Can I?

By no means did anyone officially knew of Ray's drug problem or the extent were Rahima's mental health.

I moved my eyes toward the wall again. "My brother started to um…He…."

Dang it, why could I not say it. I wanted to tell someone. I *needed* to tell someone, but it was not Riva, or Ryton I was talking about. This was my brother and sister. Ray and Rahima had been through the same crap childhood as me.

I would not tell her. Not for the sake of my pride but the sake of my brother and sisters. At least, I couldn't do it right now. Not just yet. They've kept their problems to themselves bottled up, not telling anyone for years. If they can do it, so can I.

Then Riva's words from over the years replayed in my head,

"Do not speak about family matters outside the family.

Do not talk about others the way they may talk about you.

It is not their problem to fix, and it is not their family.

If we have a problem, we will deal with it ourselves.

We do not need help, Rodrick; you just want attention."

Being here with Arcelia was making me realize how long Riva had broken me. How much I had kept to myself for the sake of stupid pride. Finally, being able to tell someone something, though, felt refreshing. This was the most peaceful I had felt in years. I could feel the tears collecting at the side of my eyes. I used my forearm to cover my face.

Do not cry in front of her; do not show weakness. Riva told me only the weak cry because they knew they could not do anything to fix their situation. And she was right.

"Rodrick," Arcelia said softly. "show me your face."

"No."

"Please?"

I breathed through my nose. "Celia, please leave me alone."

I felt the warmth from her hand leave me. Arcelia moved my forearm away. I looked up at her; my teary eyes met hers.

I let out a small laugh. "Why are you crying?"

"Why are *you* crying, Rodrick?"

Honestly, I didn't know why I was even crying in the first place. I didn't know if it was because of my family, my pain, or something else unknown to me. She moved into my lap and wiped my tears away. I did the same for her.

"I'm sorry for thinking you were just another arrogant royal."

I messed with the ends of my shirt. "Don't apologize."

"It's easier to be arrogant and rude; people don't ask questions or try to get close," I mumbled.

She hugged me tightly. "Well, too bad for you. I'm one nosey person. Now you have no choice but to be close to me."

I chuckled, hugging her back. "I guess so."

And I did not mind either.

Out of Sight

It had been four days. Four long and grueling days in this stupid bunker. No word from Queen Fayola, and no sights of Ryton, though it was not as dreadful of a thing as I thought it would be.

After Arcelia and I's talk, I felt lighter. And I got in some good sleep last night too. The sleeping dust Sandy gave me seemed to be finally working. Arcelia was at the desk, sending another letter back to her mom.

"Rodrick, I'm starting to get sick of this place," she huffed out. "I miss being outside."

She stretched her hands out to the small window above the desk.

"Maybe we could go flying?" I suggested.

She itched her bun, the sun danced on her chocolate skin. "We have to stay here."

I rubbed my eyes. "It was a suggestion. We have nothing better to do than sleep and talk."

She grumbled. "It would be nice. I could even phase us through walls instead of using the door and windows that have sensors on them."

"I forgot Umbrians could do that."

She rolled her eyes. "It's fine; I forget you're Drakonian."

I ruffled my hair. "That's because I look more Human than Drakonian."

"All of your siblings do," she addressed.

"Of course, we do," I said.

Even being one-quarter Human, those genes showed the most in my family, from our smooth skin to the softness of our hair.

If we did not tell people that we were Drakonian, they would never guess.

"Can all Umbrians become intangible?"

"Not all of us can," Arcelia dismissed.

"Why not?" I asked.

"It's like your eye color; it's an inherited trait. Some traits are rare, and some of them are common. Phasing is a rare trait for Umbrians."

So, she is a rarity? It makes a lot of sense. I've never met someone like Arcelia.

I looked out the window on the other side of the room.

"When we were at the A.J.M., I wanted to see what Drakonian wings look like in person. I was hoping you were going to fly back home," she admitted.

"That's your reason for going to fly?" I questioned.

"No, I never said I would go. But if we did, we could get some fresh air, and it'll help us clear our heads."

I studied her from afar. "Hopefully."

I watch the clouds start to grey and clump together. If we do go out, I hope it will grant us a little freedom from being stuffed in this bunker.

I leaned back on the countertop.

We finished eating lunch and somehow got back on the topic of families. This time it was Arcelia's turn again.

"I don't know why I'm so nosey about other people's lives."

She cracked a sad smile. "Maybe I like hearing about other people's families because I don't expect them to lie to me. Like mine does."

We sat quietly for another minute.

She spoke again. "My family is bizarre when it comes to affection. That stems from my grandfather. He instilled 'divide and conquer' in every aspect of his life. My mom and her siblings only care and love their children. Except for my Aunt Cal, since she has no kids of her own."

She picked at her nails. "It is really disheartening, I love my cousins, but we have always been somewhat distant. No thanks to our parents."

She shuffled her feet. "It's funny. My grandfather had four children, three girls and one boy. Now my generation, three girls and one boy. Same setup with different players. It seems that none of us will fulfill his wishes of world domination, though. How could we? We are children of war, pain, and death."

I sighed. "Don't say that, Arcelia, you're not—"

"I am," she said somberly. "There's a reason why my family is the only 'true' friends I have."

She mumbled as her eyes hardened. "My grandfather was probably a member of the Atar too. It sounds right up his alley."

Arcelia stared at the wall. "It's such a coincidence that we are both royals that have family problems, wearing masks to hide from the pain."

I shook my head. "Fate, Arcelia. It's not a coincidence."

She rolled her eyes. "I guess so."

I pointed to the Poignant Hibiscus. "That's the same plant my Mom—Maia was allergic to. How coincidental, a native Diar plant ended up in Waeven."

She stayed silent.

"You need to know you're not the only child of death in this room," I lowered my head. "I'm the reason some mad man just killed 300 people."

I gazed at a window. "You know, before I came to the meeting, I visited one of the Allos, Oracle. I saw some visions. One was of a brown-skinned girl on the floor surrounded by dark figures and blood. But I couldn't see her face because she was wearing a mask. All I could make out were her *blue eyes.*"

I looked back at Arcelia. "How much you want to bet I know what she looks like without the mask now?"

Her blue eyes were piercing. "Why did you not say anything earlier?"

I grinned. "I couldn't tell you were wearing your mask."

Silence fell over the room.

I bit my tongue. I should not have said that, but I needed to get it off my chest.

A blanket of gray clouds moved across the windows. It was raining again.

Arcelia sighed.

She raised one of her hands, casting a shadow on the floor's surface. I watched as Arcelia used her hand to twist the shadow around the hibiscus. She squeezed her hand into a strong fist. The shadow mimicked her movement and pressed itself around the plant as a snake would do to its prey. Within an instant, the plant was now a pile of broken leaves and stems. Its petals spilled onto the floor in defeat.

"That needed to be done. I have seen you stare aimlessly at the plant on and off again," she said.

"Thanks," I muttered.

She did not reply.

I walked over to the sofa, flopping down onto it gently.

We needed to fly away from this cage.

At least for a moment.

Fly Away with Me

An hour passed without Rodrick or I talking to each other. It had rained earlier, and the entire bunker felt stickier and damper than usual.

I think being in this confined space now for four days was getting to me, getting to us. I think a flight through the treetops wouldn't hurt anyone. It will be quick; we'll be out and back in before anything wrong can happen.

"Rodrick?"

"Yes?" he answered.

"Do you want to still go out?" I asked.

"Yeah, finally changed your mind?" he asked.

I nodded silently.

"Okay, give me a second," Rodrick grumbled, stretching up from the sofa.

I think both of us had had time to settle down and think. I sluggishly made my way off the bed.

I walked over to the desk, passing Rodrick. He got up and followed me.

"Before we leave, I have to make my wings," I informed him.

He shrugged. "That is fine."

I closed my eyes for a moment. "I haven't done this thing in a while; bear with me."

He hummed. "There is no rush; take your time."

I relaxed my shoulders and opened my hands, gathering shadows around me. They accumulated on my back, flaring into feathers. Soon a pair of ebony, almost angelic wings spread out from my back. I stretched my wings, trying to get used to the feeling. It took me some time to move them to my will, but Rodrick waited calmly for me to adjust.

Once I finished my stretches, I looked at Rodrick. "Your turn."

"I'm going to have to take off my shirt since there are no wing slits in the back. Will you be, okay?" he asked me mockingly.

No, but I'm going to pretend like I am.

"I will. So, you won't be wearing a shirt the whole time we're out?" I asked.

He shook his head. "No, I will. I have to make my own wing cuts."

I bobbed my head. I don't know whether to be pleased or disappointed.

He removed his shirt, showing off his shapely body. He flexed his claws out and made two quick slits in the back of his shirt.

He pulled his shirt back on. "Would you like to see them form?"

I bit my lip in excitement. "Yes, please!"

He gave a cute smile and turned around.

I held my breath.

The area between his shoulder blades shaped and restructured. His creamy skin turned into a glossy, garnet-scaled pattern. Within his back slits, a pair of wings formed, bit by bit. They got bigger and bigger as they extended outward. They seemed scaly in texture yet frill-like in appearance. Both wings started a little above his neck and ended a little above his ankles.

If he had spread them open, they would about seven feet long in wingspan.

He rotated back around to face me. "Do you like them?"

"They're gorgeous, Rodrick," I said, taking them in.

He gave me a soft smile. "So are yours, just like their owner."

"You're a mess," I beamed. "Thank you."

"You're welcome, *princesa*," he winked.

I curled my lip, ignoring his comment.

I stepped a little closer to him, reaching out for his hands. "Time for us to leave."

"If you start seeing everything in inverted colors, or my eyes gleam purple, we're fine. It's what our eyes project when this happens," I said.

"Anything else I need to know?" Rodrick asked.

"Yes. When we start phasing through the wall, spread your wings. Once we are outside, I must let go of you. The more weight I take on when I phase, the weaker I get."

He gave me a thumbs up.

I took a deep breath and closed my eyes, then opened them. The colors around us inverted as I guided us through the stone wall of the bunker.

Once we were outside, my eyes reverted to their normal blue. I let go of Rodrick's hands, and we were tangible again. Rodrick's wings flapped with a faint whoosh.

In the view of the sun, the crimson scales glistened. They were even prettier than before.

"Where to now, Celia?" he asked.

"You haven't been here before, right?"

He shook his head. "No."

I smiled. "You have been missing out," I held out my hand. "Would you like to take a tour of one of the best rainforests on the planet?"

He slid his hand into mine, pulling me close. "I would love to."

My face got warm. "Okay, let's get started."

At first, I tried to give a tour; however, that ended as quickly as it started because of Rodrick playing around and me not really taking the tour thing seriously. The sky was open and empty for us to navigate through as we raced through the treetops. But man, Rodrick was fast. And I mean *fast.*

Me, not being as fast as him, found myself out of breath and leaning on trees for support every 7 seconds.

"Celia? Where are you, *princesa*?"

I raised my hand dimly. "I'm here."

I felt his strong hand grip mine and pull me up. I grabbed onto his forearm for more support.

He chuckled. "Are you tired?"

I breathed out. "Yes, very."

He pulled me into his chest. "Maybe I should find a place to lay you down."

I tiredly pushed him away.

"No. I, I am fine," I heaved out.

Wow, I really didn't know I was so winded.

His arms shifted to carry me. I would have protested if I did not feel like I had run a marathon. I pulled my wings back, so he could hold me better.

He glanced at me. "Do you want to go back already?"

I shook my head. "No, we can find a treetop to lay on."

He pulled me closer to his chest. "Do I have to tell you to hold on?"

I grabbed his shirt like a needy child. "No."

With a single flap of his wings, he was off.

The rushing wind hit my face. Rain droplets sprinkled on me, making it hard to see. I turned my head against his body to stop the force of it. In seconds, the bursts of cooling air and water contained.

Rodrick put me in one of the treetops.

"That was fast," I acknowledged.

He looked down, a smirk on his face. "I had to slow down for you. I *can* go faster."

He plopped his body next to mine.

I cast him a sideways glance. "Why do you have to tease?"

He rolled onto his back, looking at the sky. "Do you not like it?"

I turned my head, not answering him at first.

I looked up at the sky. "I just wanted to know why you were doing it."

He huffed. "Because I want to."

The stars started to dot the purplish sky.

"Celia."

"Yes?"

He paused for a second. "How long do you think we'll be able to hide from him?"

I stayed quiet. I didn't know what to say.

All I knew was that I would be scared when he did find us.

I reached out for his hand, and he grabbed mine.

"I don't know, but let's enjoy the peace while we can."

CHAPTER FOURTEEN

RUNNING OUT OF TIME

Our swords clashed, interlocking. Our blades were sliding against one another. I stepped back.

Then I felt it.

Their sword was going through my body. I watched as my blood dripped down. I gripped their cloak, pulling the hood off their head.

I was shocked to see her painted face. Her jet-black curls sprang around her alabaster face. Her amethyst eyes stared into my soul.

"One must die."

Lady Death pulled her sword out of my limp body.

"Lu—"

"Rodrick!"

My eyes burst open; my body shot up.

A dream? That was a dream.

Lady Death was in it. Dreaming of the Acolyte of Death is *never* a good thing.

"Rodrick?"

My head followed the sound of the voice.

"Arcelia," I said, panting.

Wait, why am I panting?

"Are you all, right? You were starting to breathe hard."

I wiped the sweat off my face. "I'm fine."

It was late afternoon and Arcelia, and I decided to take a quick nap before we would go flying again. It was nice the first time yesterday, and one more flight wouldn't do us harm. At least, that is what I told Celia to convince her to go again.

I got up from the bed and went to get a drink.

I shook my head. "I can't stay here, not anymore. I can't keep hiding from him. I don't know what is happening to me."

"What do you mean?" she inquired.

"Arcelia," I turned to face her. "It has been *too* quiet for too long...it's been five days and nothing...nothing."

She came over to me, softly pushing my hair out of my face. "Rodrick, take it easy. What's wrong?"

The sound of thunderous clouds rang from the sky. "I don't know. I need to leave. I have this feeling that he's close. Something is coming soon."

She cupped my face. "Rodrick, calm down. We're okay. You know we can't leave, well not like yesterday's flight. The safest and best thing for us—for you to do is to stay here."

The sky thickened to a gray color.

She combed her fingers delicately through my hair. "I know how you feel. I'm scared too."

A rapid pain traveled up my arm. I winced, moving away from Arcelia.

She quickly followed me.

"I'm fine," I reassured her.

Another sharp pain jabbed through my arm. I pressed my Emblem. My vision went blurry.

I started to see visions of

Islands
Chaparrals
Rainforests

Underwater
Water, water, water
Gold on gold
Submarine
Crest of Time

I released my forearm.

I slid down to the floor. "He has completed the Crest."

"What!?"

I looked up and met Arcelia's worried face. "I saw the Crest. He has all of the pieces."

She stayed silent.

"He may know where we are, but I may know where he is. I think he's on a submarine, somewhere near the Chaparrals, where the gateway is."

Arcelia crossed her arms. "The Chaparrals? Rodrick, you need like three background checks to get anywhere near one of their islands."

I hold my shaky hands. "I know; however, they have some unguarded and uninhabited areas. Lucky for us, the gateway is on one of them."

"The gateway?" she questioned.

"It's a temple ruin. The temple was made for the purpose of time travel, which is where the Crest was created too. Though to the normal person they're just big boulders," I explained.

"Oh."

The thunder boomed louder now.

"I feel like an idiot," I said, rubbing my face.

Arcelia sat down next to me, leaning her head on my shoulder. Shooting pains were still raged through my arm.

"So, what do we do now?" I asked.

She groaned. "I don't know."

"If I go to him, that's a problem. If he comes here, that's a problem..."

She gripped my left arm. "Rodrick—" Another clap of thunder shook through the sky.

Step, step, step.

"Wait," I whispered. "I hear footsteps,"

I rose to my feet and eyed the door. Arcelia joined me. I held my finger to my lips. She stayed silent.

Step, step, step, step, step, step.

The footsteps stopped.

The door busted open.

Men in black armor came rushing in. I moved quickly to the coffee table, throwing it in their direction. I hit two of them. Three more men rushed toward me. One tried to punch me, but I sidestepped, grabbing his wrist and throwing him at another guy. I suddenly felt someone's foot sink into the back of my knee and another in my shoulder. I fell to the floor but rolled away before anyone could pin me down. I stood up, ignoring the pain. I slammed my fist into one of them with full force. I heard a bone crack.

An arm grabbed around my neck and yanked back. I protracted my claws.

"I would not try to fight this one."

I glanced sideways. In the corner of my eye, I saw Celia with a knife at her neck.

"She's not what we are here for, so ending the Princess's life will not be hard."

I looked into her eyes, and they spoke to me.

I smirked. "You should be more worried about yourself than her."

The man opened his mouth to speak, then Arcelia phased through his arm. My foot crushed my restrainer's own, and he backed off. I elbowed him in the stomach.

"Rodrick!" I glanced at Arcelia. She rushed over to me and reached out for my hand. I catch her, and we phase through the ground.

She guided us out through a wall and to a lower level where the SUV was parked.

"I got the keys, get in the driver's side," she commanded.

I rushed to the door, pulling it open.

I backed us out of the parking space and out of the cave.

We passed by four armored military trucks.

I cursed heavily under my breath. They had been staking us out. As we headed out, three of the cars came charging after us.

"Celia, do you know any way we can lose them?" I questioned, making sharp turns on the rugged terrain.

"Just keep driving straight, as straight as you can," she answered.

She made her way to the back of the truck.

"Can you let the top down?" I pulled down on the handle of the roof and twisted it clockwise. The top of the SUV began to slide down.

"Thanks!" She yelled at me.

Through the rearview mirror, I saw her conjuring different shapes and shadowy objects, charging them at the cars behind us.

I rewound to the front.

A fallen tree was in our path. *Crap.*

I whipped the car to the left, nearly hitting the tree and driving over a few tree stumps.

There was a loud thump and scream from the back.

"RODRICK!"

I glimpsed in the mirror. "Sorry, there was a tree."

"Well, if you were paying attention—"

A loud thud came from the back. The car behind us was hitting our rear end.

"Rodrick hit the gas!"

"I know!" I hammered my foot on the accelerator. The truck zoomed through the jungle.

Rain poured from the sky.

I heard Arcelia moving around in the back.

"You're welcome," I sneered.

Shots rang out.

Arcelia gasped. "They're shooting at us!?"

I looked in the side mirror. A man out the back window of the car was holding a machine gun.

Shots rang out again. This time, one hit the side door of the car.

"Celia, get down!"

"Trust me, I'm already ahead of you!" she screamed. "Why are they shooting!? They need you alive!"

They fired another round of shots, one of the bullets hitting the glass of my right-side mirror. Others were denting various parts of the car.

"Yeah, but they don't need the car running or you are alive."

She crawled her way to the front. "Well, they're doing a bad job."

I glanced at her, gripping the steering wheel. "Do you want them to do a *decent job*?"

A tire on my right made a brash popping sound.

"They shot a tire!" Arcelia quickly put up the car's roof. "Wonderful!"

I swerved the car a bit. "Arcelia, you were more helpful when you were back there."

"You think I'm gonna fight them when they are shooting *at me*!?"

I ignored her, complaining. "Can you make a shield around us?"

"No," Arcelia responded. "the car is moving too fast for me to conjure any shadows that big."

Bullets penetrated the SUV's roof. I made another sharp turn.

"Rodrick, if I hit my head again, I swear I might kill *you.*"

"Fine with me!" I pressed on the gas harder.

The rain was coming down harder, and the trees became denser and denser. As we sped down the path, I saw another fallen tree blocking our way.

Great.

An idea popped in my head. "Hey, Arcelia, can you phase us through that tree?"

She leaned forward to check the distance. Another round of shots rang through, and her head at once ducked back down. "I don't know. There is a seventy-five percent chance that I can't."

"Those odds are good enough for me," I said as a bullet flew through the other side view mirror.

"We can't drive on and hope they simply run out of bullets. Especially since *they are aiming at you.*"

She twisted her head back. "All right, I'll try!"

Another tire burst, *how many guns do they have?*

She grabbed my arm and the truck. "Here goes nothing!"

No Time Left

I slowed the car down. It was pouring even harder than before. "I think we've lost them for now."

Arcelia was heaving hard. Her face covered in sweat.

"There's no way we can go back," she murmured.

"Ryton has found us. They probably have been searching for us for a while," I said.

She looked at her fingers, disheartened.

I kept my eyes focused forward. "I'm going to have to face him."

"Not alone," she whispered.

I gazed at her.

"I want you to be as safe as much as I do for myself," I told her.

"You didn't really think I was gonna leave now, did you?" she questioned.

I smiled gently. "I guess not. I was hoping you would leave, though. I don't need you getting hurt."

"Seeing that they tried to kill me, I don't think they would let me just leave Waeven," she droned.

She had a point. She was stuck with me, whether I liked it or not.

I focused on the road ahead of me. "How do we get out of this rainforest?"

"Continue straight; we'll reach the main road shortly."

I loosened my grip on the wheel. "How do you know?"

"The rainforest is fully encircled by road. If you keep straight, you will find your way out."

I pressed the gas again, thankful that the car was still running well.

"Rodrick, does Queen Riva know where the temple is?"

"Yes, she does," I replied.

"Maybe there is a way I can help."

I glanced at her. "How?"

"If I can get to my mom, she can get to Queen Riva."

"How do you plan on getting us across the sea?" I asked.

She bit her lip. "We have to drive to the docks."

"Why?"

"If I have my days counted, the docks correctly should be closed today, including the stores around it. So, nobody should be there," she enlightened me.

"We are going to need some things; food, new clothes, a map, a track phone, maybe and a boat."

I grasped the steering wheel. "Makes sense."

The rain started to lift. "If everything is closed, how do you plan on getting these things?"

She chuckled. "By becoming intangible, of course."

"You plan on stealing everything?" I peeked down at my arm; the pain had stopped, but the Emblem was still glowing.

She spun away from me. "I consider it to be borrowing without asking."

I glanced at her. "Seriously?"

Well, if she's okay with it, so am I.

"I'm kidding."

Oh.

She opened the center console and pulled out a box. "This box has 2,500 Boscan dollars in it."

I raised my eyebrows.

"It's for emergencies," she answered.

I slowed down as the shrubbery began to lessen. "Arcelia, you don't have to do this. You can stay here and hide in a store or something."

"Rodrick, I'm not leaving you, and I'm sick of hiding," she shut the console. "What will we do when we get to this island?"

I ruffled my hair. "I don't know. I simply know that we are going there."

I watched my arm glow. "Please, trust me on this, and we have to go there."

She stared at my glowing forearm then out the window. "All right, I trust you."

CHAPTER FIFTEEN

THE QUEEN FEARED BY MOST

I sipped my glass of water. Far too angry to enjoy the taste of red wine. *He has my son.*

That worthless man has my son. No harm was to come to my children when they were out of my care. None. Not a scratch, a bruise, nothing. Despite this, look at where my rushed trust and venal pride have gotten me, alone in a castle, where I sat fearing for all my children's lives. *How dare he.*

I took another sip of my water.

My children were all I had. They are all I have. I started at the chair in front of me. I wanted to burn it. I wanted to burn everything that the monster touched in my presence. Burn down the whole castle if I must.

He would burn for this. No one touched my children. No one.

I took another sip.

There was a knock at the door. I clenched my glass. "I said to leave me alone."

"Queen Riva?"

I put my glass down.

It was him—that *traitor.*

"You may enter," I said in a firm voice. General Maves walked in and bowed.

"Sit down and close the door behind you," I said.

He did as I told.

. I picked my glass again. "I wanted some more time to think alone."

"Then you should not have invited me in, Your Highness," he added with grit in his words.

You pouco de merda. "I suppose you are correct. Why are you here?"

He leaned his body back in the chair. "Well, to speak to you, my Queen."

This dirty little—

"About what?" I took a drink from my glass.

"About Prince Rod— "

"No."

He looked at me, confused. "Pardon?"

"General Maves. I do not wish to speak to you about my son."

He opened his mouth.

"Close your mouth and stay silent. I am not finished."

He quickly shut it.

I glimpsed at my half-empty glass. "I'm not surprised that you like to be Ryton's *puto*. I know you are the snitch who has been telling him everything that happens in the Castle."

I took another sip. "Am I correct?"

He clenched his jaw, looking more nervous by the second. He knew what was going to happen.

"I've had doubts about you for so long. You fooled me for quite some time. I was wondering when he would replace the last informer, though it took him a couple of months."

His face tensed, I as hoped, with fear.

I finished my glass.

"Fool me once, shame on you. Fool me twice, shame on me. Take my son..."

I pressed my claws into the glass, breaking it in my hand. I watched the blood drip down.

I glared at Maves. "Now, how would you like me to shatter you?"

CHAPTER SIXTEEN

TIME WITH TIME

"Rodrick, Rodrick."

I opened my eyes. "Tempus? Is that you?"

I saw where I was, on the floor of one of her many solariums.

"Yes, it is."

I got up and turned toward her voice. Her appearance had changed since I last saw her. She was still tall. Her face now had freckles. Her eyes held more of a bronze color. Her hair was short and magenta. The most dramatic change was the golden mechanical wings on her back and gold mechanical arms and hands.

"I am at Taporis?" I inquired.

"Yes, but only through cognition," she responded.

"I am here mentally."

"Correct. Physically…" she swirled her hands to create a portal screen.

I peered into it, seeing myself lying on a metallic floor. My eyes were shut; my breathing was slow.

"…You're on Ryton's submarine," she finished.

I froze.

That was right, and we were captured. Memories started to come back to me. Arcelia and I drove to the dock, where Ryton's men were waiting for us. They had the whole island surrounded. We were not going to make it off, no matter where we ran. They knew we would try to jet off by boat. I admit it was an amateur plan, but it was all we had.

I put my head down. "I couldn't stop him. He knew where we would be, hell, he knows more about this stupid mark than I do."

She placed her hand on my shoulder. "You will be fine, my child."

I shook my head. "No, Tempus. I may be fine, but so many others are not because of Ryton. People's lives depend on me, and I don't even know how to stop him! I had years to think of something! I knew this day might come, and still, I did nothing!"

She moved her hand back. "Are you angry with me? Do you think I am the cause of this?"

I shook my head. "No. I am mad, but I don't have any reason to be mad at you. You haven't done anything."

"Maybe that is why you should be mad," she said.

I focused my eyes on the floor.

She exhaled. "For millions of years, I have sat back and watched you, creatures, destroy everything repeatedly. Even now, when my own Acolytes needed me the most, I was not there."

I shrugged. "At least I turned out fine, for the most part."

She grinned. "I agree. Now for the important part."

Tempus clapped her hands, and three torsion clocks materialized before her.

"I knew you were coming, so I went and picked out these clocks beforehand."

The clocks had names on them: Arcelia Ellora Phacadé, Rodrick Darren Purcill, and *Ryton Darrel Purcill.*

I frowned at Ryton's clock.

I stared hard at Ryton and Arcelia's clocks.

"Theirs are not moving," I gulped.

Tempus gave me a reassuring smile. "Do not worry, child, and they are both alive. I just did some tweaking to the clocks."

"Arcelia is alive," I murmured. "I knew I shouldn't have wrapped her up in all this."

"She chose to go with you. It was her choice, not yours," Tempus said.

"I know this may be a dumb question, but is his plan ever going to work?"

Tempus scoffed. "No. Ryton wants to travel back in time, which is impossible."

"Is it impossible for us too?" I asked.

She shook her head. "Not necessarily. I am the physical embodiment of time. Since I was born, the time has always moved forward. Time can never go back. That is why you can only stop and speed up time, but not reverse it. Yet there is still a way to go back. It is exceedingly, difficult, and extremely dangerous."

Her eyebrow knitted together. "The only way to do this is by going through a parallel universe where the point in time you are aiming for is not past, but present. The problem is not the ability to travel, yet the abuse of the ability."

So, he could go back, kind of.

"This has happened before?" I asked.

She agrees. "Yes, three times. Each time due to the greed of a mortal. They open too many portals, too many parallel realities. It causes rifts in the space-time continuum, causing...what do you Earthlings call it? Doomsday?"

I clenched my fist. "If this has happened before, why have we not heard about it?"

She looked at the clocks and then back to me. "Due to the rifts, I, Hapesire, Vitae, and Mors return everything to its first state."

"You mean, you reset time?"

She shook her head. "No. We reset everything, time, space, life, and death. It is like a rebirth of all things. It is quite painful to do. But then again, I must do painful things. A lot of painful things."

For the first time, I saw hurt in her eyes.

"Tempus…"

"Back to these," she changed the subject. "You know of my sibling Mors' Acolyte?"

"Yes, Lady Death, Luluona."

"Correct."

Tempus took hold of Ryton's clock. "I, along with Mors and Lady Death, agreed some time ago on the subject of Ryton. We knew he would come back and try to disrupt Earth. So, we tried to see who would deal with him. Usually, my brother is the one to deal with these types of problems, yet this one had my Acolyte directly attached to it."

She reached out for my hands. "Rodrick, we decided that you would be the one to decide Ryton's fate."

My eyes widened. "Me?"

"Yes, this has a lot to do with you," she set Ryton's clock down. "I have seen visions of the future beyond now. From what I have seen, you will have to choose between your head and your heart."

Her gaze shifted to Arcelia's clock. "And not merely for Ryton's future."

I looked at Arcelia's clock. "Why didn't you tell me earlier?"

"You did not need that much time," she said.

I furrowed my eyebrows. "So, this was the perfect time to tell me?"

Her eyes narrowed. "This was the *only* time to tell you. It may not seem like it to you, Rodrick, but I understand the powers of time and how to manipulate them to my will far greater than you or Ryton."

I could tell she was getting irritated.

I may be hot-headed, but I was not stupid enough to pick a fight with a God.

"Okay. I am not saying you don't know. I just don't know if the choice I make will be the choice you predicted."

"Rodrick, you will make the right choice," she reassured.

I moved away from her. "Thanks, I guess."

"Rodrick, when you go back, you are going to find out more things that will make you angry. Know that everything that will happen was fated to happen at that time. Not before, not after. Forgive me in advance."

I sucked air through my teeth. What difference would it make if I forgave her or not?

What more did I expect of her? It's always been like this, vague answers to import, and detailed questions.

Well, just as Tempus said, this is my fate.

I placed my hands in my pockets. "Okay, so how do I get back?"

She walked over to me and kissed the top of my head.

"Continue on your path to greatness. Until next time, my child."

She raised a hand. A gold ring formed around my feet. Her eyes glowed white as a small wind whipped around my body.

Everything went black.

Not in the Clear

Tempus' words rang in my ears; *"You will be the one to decide his fate,"* I reopened my eyes. I was in a glass cell. My body was leaned against a pillar. I stared at the Emblem. It was still glowing. I touched it, trying to see if I could use it, but nothing happened.

What was I supposed to do?

"You're finally awake," I spun my body toward the weak voice behind me.

"Arcelia?"

She was in an all-glass cell like mine. Her body was propped up against the wall next to me. Her hair was tangled. Her face and body were bruised. I saw nothing but pain in her eyes.

"Are you okay?" she sounded so frail.

I touched the glass. "Are *you okay?* What did they do to you?"

She hugged her body tightly, refusing to meet my eyes.

Her eyes started to water. "I...nothing."

"They didn't do anything."

I could hear her voice starting to crack. "You've been lying there for a while, so they came to question me about it."

"Arcelia—"

She turned her head away from me. "I didn't know what to tell them, you weren't waking up. No matter what I tried."

Now I was pissed.

I balled my fist and slammed it against our connecting wall. It made Arcelia flinch.

Looking at her made my heart hurt. "I wish I could hug you."

She gave me a dry laugh. "So do I."

Gods, this is all my fault.

"I'm so sorry."

"It's not your fault, Rodrick. Where were you?"

I exhaled. "I talked to Tempus."

"Really?" her eyes brightened with hope.

"She—"

The sound of a door opening cut my sentence short.

Arcelia looked at me with worry.

"It's okay," I tried to assure her.

"Prince Rodrick, you are finally awake."

I moved my head towards the voice.

It came from a lean man with dark blonde hair. His left hand was missing, and his face was smug. Behind him were several other men, all of them dressed in black military uniforms and heavily armed. He whispered to one of the men. A man walked over to Arcelia's cell and opened the locked door. Arcelia stiffened in the corner. The man remained quiet as he made his way to her.

"Hey! What the—"

The man pulled out a gun. Arcelia and I froze.

"Prince Rodrick?" The blond man said.

"If you do not shut up and comply with the things, I said," his eyes fell on Arcelia. "her head will earn a nice hole in it. Don't try my patience. Do you have a problem with that?"

I gritted my teeth.

He sneered. "I didn't think you would. Get up."

I stood, peering at Arcelia.

"Rodrick—"

"Quiet, shadow girl," the blond man barked.

He refocused his attention back to me and opened my cell door. The men behind him adjusted their weapons.

I whistled. "Are those toys all for me?"

The blond man gestured to Arcelia. "I can still shoot the girl. Come here."

I dropped the smirk and cautiously made my way to the door.

"Nice to have to have a prince wrapped around my finger."

I eyed him.

Like how Ryton has you wrapped around his? I wanted to say it so badly, but for Arcelia's sake, I kept silent.

He cuffed my hands with a pair of rigid handcuffs. He pressed a switch on the cuffs. Instantly, it felt like an extra two-hundred pounds had been added to my wrist. My body dropped a bit at the straining weight. I glanced back at Arcelia. Her eyes were fiery, with tears running down her face.

I gave her a small smile. *I'll be okay, promise.*

I could feel the sweat running down my face. The cuffs felt like they were about to tear my arms off. I followed the man and his team down the hallways in silence. It was dimly lit and eerily calm. The smell of ocean water and fish surrounded us.

I knew they were taking me to Ryton. What would I do when I finally saw him? Should I kill him on the spot, then destroy the Crest of Time? I stared at his men. What would I do with them? I should beat the Crest of Time first, then fight him. I could take him like that.

Arcelia.

The man holding a gun to her never came with us. He would kill her if I tried anything stupid.

"We are here, boy."

I looked up at the solemn grey door in front of me. This is it.

May the hands of Tempus guide me.

Plan with No Reason

The room I entered was dark. There were no windows or lights on. The only light in the room was coming from my arm. Even so, I could see the venomous green eyes of Ryton.

Ryton was wearing all-black and standing in front of a desk. His skin was covered in scales, with small horns protruding from his arms and face. His hair was a duller red with silver strands.

He had a pair of extensive wings that sprouted slightly above his shoulder blades. His claws were tapping the desk, and his green eyes were glaring at me. He flipped the switch to the light on his desk.

I scowled. "Tempus says hi."

He clamped his fist together as he rose from his seat. "That is the first thing you say to your father?"

"You are not my father, Ryton."

He clicked his tongue. "King Ryton to you. It seems your mother did not teach you respect."

"At least I can say she was there," I spat.

He grinned. "Now, this is no way to act. Especially when your little girlfriend has a bullet was waiting to pierce her skull."

I closed my mouth in anger.

"Good boy."

He sat back down in his chair. "You and your mother both seem better when quiet."

He gestured to a seat. "Sit down."

I remained standing.

"Suit yourself," he said smugly. "I know those cuffs are heavy. I wanted to give you get some relief. I had those cuffs made solely for you. Think of it as my first gift to you."

"What do you plan on doing?" I asked.

Ryton grinned viciously. "What a smart question, dear boy. You see, the world is tainted. So much is wrong with it, with every race on this planet. Even I have imperfections to an extent."

I stared at the madman as he continued.

"The world needs to be reborn. A place where wealth and material value are not the highest priority. Where every person knows their place and solitary purpose to society. A world where if someone is disobedient, they are eradicated. There are no warnings or penalties where I control the future and present. Where the only thing the world will fear is the thought of time forever in my corner."

I shook my head. "Well, first, you're crazy, and second, it won't work."

"Oh?" he leered at me, never breaking eye contact. "Why not?"

I heaved, trying to battle with the weights of the cuffs on me.

He leaned back in his chair. "Is it because the Crest is not completed? Because it is. Is it because I do not have the Key of Tempus? Because I do. Is it because I do not know where to go? Because we are heading there right now."

He laughed. "You said earlier that Tempus said hello to me? Did Tempus also tell you how my intentions would fail?"

I bit hard on my tongue.

He pulled out the Crest of Time from inside his desk, setting it down on top. "Is it not a beauty?"

If I bit down on my tongue any harder, blood would start flowing.

"Why so quiet, Rodrick? Thinking of what to do? Hm? What are you going to do, Rodrick? Are you going to kill me?"

My claws pressed against the cuffs.

"If I die," he pointed at the door. "my men will see and will not hesitate to kill her too."

I said nothing.

"What are you to do?" he taunted. "Are you going to let me live?"

He got up and began circling his desk. "You think I have all of my chips betting on you and this old relic?"

I stood weakly.

"You think I did not have other strategies in the works?" he shook his head. "I thought the Acolyte of Death was clueless."

He scoffed. "You honestly believe that for sixteen years, I was only going around trying to find these pieces? I've had plans since the day I was 'thrown' into prison. You're lucky this one is the only one I need you alive for. The thing is, when I start something, I always finish it. No matter how long it takes me."

My claws scratched the palms of my hands.

He sneered at my long claws. "Itching to fight me, boy?"

He and I both knew the answer to that question. If it weren't for these cuffs, undeniably, I would. With the agonizing weight of the cuffs on me, it was a shock I had not fallen to the ground.

"We have less than an hour before we hit the shore of the Chaparrals. If you cooperate, so many peoples' lives will be spared. You would not want your sisters and girlfriend to die because of your stubbornness?"

I retracted my claws. Sweat completely covered my face. It was hard to breathe.

Ryton's lips curled into a grin. "That's what I thought."

He sat down in his chair again. "You may leave unless there is something you want to say."

I staggered around to the door. Every step was becoming harder and harder to take.

"Ryton," I turned my head over my shoulder, breathing out. "your 'perfect' world is not happening."

He chuckled. "Who is to say that it hasn't already begun?"

CHAPTER SEVENTEEN

NEVER MADE IT

"One hour before we hit the shore," was all I was able to get from Rodrick when he returned.

I started to panic. What is Ryton going to do with me after? They only needed me alive for so long. What more of Rodrick? I cannot run or escape because we were miles below the surface. I could barely lift myself. There was no point in crying or screaming or shouting. I couldn't blame Rodrick; I couldn't blame my mom or even Ryton. I stubbornly got myself into this mess, and there was no way I could get myself out.

"Arcelia?"

I snapped out of my thoughts and shifted my head in Rodrick's direction.

"I can't stop him."

"I can try to kill him, but" he breathed out heavily. "will it stop this? He is not the only one in the Atar pulling strings, I know it. What will stop them? I can't go around trying to kill every person I deem evil or wrong."

"If you did that," I said in a whisper. "you would be exactly like Ryton."

He groaned. "We need a miracle."

"You mean Mir?"

He gave me a dry laugh. "I don't think any of Vitae's Votaries will interfere with this. It's not like I can contact them. I'm not their Acolyte, and my stupid arm is making my powers useless."

"There must be something we can do," I tried. "The only question is what?"

He snorted. "I— "

The lights went off. The sounds of alarms rang out.

"What happened!?" Rodrick shouted.

What in the world!?

—Wait, that smell.

Posy Flowers?

I know who it is!

"Rodrick!"

"What!?"

"Cover your head and get on the floor!" I yelled.

"Why?"

"Just do it, please!"

I ducked and covered my head after I heard his body hit the floor. Something big knocked on the right side of the submarine.

Everything shifted. There were screams and shouts echoing through the hallways. It was like there was a war going on all around me. Gunshots rang throughout my cell. Sounds of a horse's gallop clattered through the walls. The thumping of bodies hitting the ground, boomed through the area.

Then as suddenly as it started, the chaos stopped.

It was deadly silent.

There was a new smell, blood. And a lot of it. I saw a black mist seeping through the seams of the walls. *It is her.*

A thud came from somewhere in front of me.

"Who the hell— "

"Rodrick, please relax. I know who is doing this."

He went quiet. "It's you."

Who is he talking to?

Another thud came. Then another, then another.

The sound of glass shattering pulled my attention. The lights flickered on. I steadily rose, using the wall for support. When I looked up, I saw her astride a black horse.

Lady Death.

She was wearing a leather jumpsuit. Her black hood covered her painted face. Her white skin glowed under the dimming lights. In her hand, she held a flaming teal and purple scythe. She smiled at me before she and the horse phased into the wall next to me.

I sighed, feeling grateful. "Thank you, my Lady."

CHAPTER EIGHTEEN

FINAL TIDE

I got up calmly and saw that the front glass of my cell was shattered. Arcelia's mirror was broken too. Her eyes were fixed on the shattered glass.

"Arcelia," I called.

She turned to me, wearily. "We got to leave."

She meekly phased through our connecting wall. I blinked.

"I thought you were too weak to use any of your abilities."

Something rocked the sub again, throwing us off our balance.

I steadied both of us before we could fall on the floor.

"I am but, Lady Death. She gave me some strength. I will explain later. Right now, we need to get off this thing before it sinks."

I gazed into her eyes. "Okay since you know what is happening, lead the way."

We hardly made it through two hallways when I stopped.

Arcelia, who was holding my hand, turned to me. "What's wrong?"

"We cannot leave," I gazed at my arm then to her. "The Crest. He still has it."

She released my hand. "Do you know where it is?"

"Yes, I do."

"As stupid as I am, I still don't want to leave you," she said.

I pulled her into a hug. Once again, the sub lurched to the side, making us stumble.

"I got to go," I said into her hair.

"You don't have to go alone," Arcelia murmured.

"Celia, that thing needs to be destroyed."

She cupped my face. "I understand, and I'm coming with you, okay? I said we're in this together, and I meant it."

I smiled. "Thank you."

I leaned in close. "but I won't let you kill yourself for my sake."

"Rod—"

I grabbed her left arm and pressed her pressure point under her jaw, and she passed out. I picked her up and started running. I ran around until I found an empty office. I laid her body on the sofa in the room.

I kissed the top of her head. "I'll come back, *minha princesa.* I promise."

I closed the door and headed for Ryton. I made it to the door and kicked it in. It was empty—no Ryton. Something sat in the center of his desk, the Crest. It was too easy. I took a step forward, and a sharp pain sliced through my arm. I cradled it against my chest. I glimpsed the Crest. It felt like it was repelling me like it did not want me to come closer.

I scanned the room. "Ryton, where are you?"

A boot pressed into my back; I hit the ground.

"This was what you were scheming?" he growled.

He dug his boot deeper into my back.

I grimaced in pain.

He laughed. "You sound so weak."

Something in me snapped. I pushed myself off the ground, which made Ryton's body stagger back.

He smiled wickedly. "Your eyes are gold. Perfect."

Ryton moved to kick me, and I grabbed his foot, throwing him into a glass cabinet. He struggled to get up. A sharp pain moved through my whole body, causing me to kneel.

He chuckled. "That is right, kneel before your King."

I watched him walk over to a darkened corner of the room. Meanwhile, I tried to muscle up the strength to stand back up.

"Do you know what this is, boy?"

He came back holding a spear. The spear had small symbols inscribed on it. Its head was adorned with a gold pendulum clock and two spinning rings. Right in the middle of the watch was a jagged blade. The sub rocked roughly.

He used the spear to balance himself. "Each God has a weapon or tool passed down to each Acolyte. Lady Death has the scythe. For Hapesire, a poleaxe. For Vitae, a staff. For you, this spear."

My eyes widen.

He laughed. "What? Did Tempus not tell you? What do you even know about the God you serve?"

I slowly rose to my feet.

He gripped the spear in his hands. "The Acolyte of Time, struggling to stand in front of an old Drakonian man."

"Ryton, you are so full of it," I spat out.

He frowned.

"Enough talking," he slammed the spearhead into the floor.

The spear, my arm, and the Crest all glowed vigorously. A beam of light connected us, making a triangle. The whole submarine began to shake. The lights in the room switched on and off like crazy. The sub shook, even more, causing me to fall back to the floor.

"Wait, this isn't supposed to happen yet!"

I watched the Ryton. He was…worried?

I tried my best to stand up. My head was woozy. I ignored it, charging at him. I protracted my claws and went for his chest. He managed to move out of the way.

"So, you are going to—"

"You talk too much," I said, throwing two punches. He grabbed my left fist, trying to twist it back. I kicked him in the knee; he went down. I aimed for his face, but he caught my foot. The sub dove, and we toppled, losing our footing.

I sank my claws into the wall and pulled myself up. There was a big crashing sound, and everything went up in the air. I turned my head to see Ryton's foot aiming for my face. I grabbed his foot with my empty hand and tried to throw him. The submarine spun, and the back of Ryton's other boot hit my neck. I winced in pain, freeing his other foot.

I tore my claws out of the wall, lashing at him. My eyes went to the disregarded spear. I started after it when Ryton sank a claw into the back of my left leg, dragging me back. I screamed in agony, striking him with my right leg. It took two more kicks to the face for him to release me. I reached out and grabbed the spear aiming for—

Everything went white.

Before Time was Space

I was placed in an all-white room. The spear was held tightly in my right hand. I could feel the blood and sweat dripping from my body. *No!* Where the hell was Ryton? I was so close to ending all of it! My grip on the spear tightened.

"Hello, Rick."

I spun around and readied myself to aim. Standing there was a stocky girl with creamy skin and beaming brown eyes.

My tense demeanor relaxed. "Hello, Caro?"

She smiled wide, showing off her braces. She was wearing a baggy pink sweater, dark jeans, and white heels. Her lips were a deep purple color. Her hair was a mix of blues, purples, and pinks and in two buns.

I walked up to her. "Where am I? And why are you here?"

"Stop," she held her hand in front of me. "did you not notice anything different?"

I was still a bit tense, but Caro, for some odd reason, wasn't. That gave me a sign that wherever I was, was safe. I knew if I answered her questions, she'd answer mine.

I took a minute to examine her. "You're wearing contacts instead of glasses?"

She crossed her arms. "Try higher."

"Oh, your hair is in those spacey balls."

She groaned loudly. "No, you idiot!"

I laughed. "I know, you changed your hair color again."

She huffed. "Yes, but this is my natural hair color, or um, colors. And the hairstyle is called space buns."

"It fits you."

"As it should," her demeanor changed.

Caro straightened her posture. "Hello, Miss Milky."

I whirled around to see whom she was talking to. It was a towering, purple-skinned woman. She had dark blue hair with dusky pink and purple tips. The left side of her head was shaved. She had about ten piercings on her face and ears. She was wearing a silver, regal, space ensemble. With all of that, the most exciting thing about her appearance was her galaxy-filled irises and two pairs of arms.

"Umm...hi. Where am I, and why am I here?"

She narrowed her eyes. "You are the Acolyte of Tempus that is causing me a problem?"

I peered at Caro for an explanation. "Rick, this is Miss Milky."

"Milky is fine," she answered.

"Milky is the embodiment of galaxies and creator of cosmos. She is the only child of Hapesire. Plus, my boss, caretaker, and guardian," Caro finished.

Milky chuckled. "Thank you for the introduction, Caro. You may leave now."

Caro bowed and then glanced at me.

Was she going to leave me with space eyes?

She seemed to have read my mind as she spoke again. "Actually ma'am, I mean, Milky, I would like to stay, please."

Milky puffed. "All right."

I looked at Milky. "So, now am I in trouble with you?"

She raised an eyebrow. "Is this how you talk to all higher entities?"

I stared at her. "Yes."

She shook her head. "Never mind. We do not have the time. You and I have a problem to deal with."

"How so?"

Milky stared at me. "You are trying to travel back in time."

I scoffed. "Not by choice."

"Yes, I am aware. It is the reason we are here," she gestured to the white space around us.

"This," she continued. "is a 'buffer zone' of sorts between dimensions and universes."

"Since you and the Demon King tried to go back in time, you landed here," Caro clarified.

I furrowed my eyebrows. "Huh? How is that possible?"

Caro began. "You know about one of the Chaparrals' islands being the time gate, right?"

"Yes, I know," I said.

"If the Spear, Key, and Crest of Time are together at the proper ritual area to perform time travel, it takes you through the buffer zone to the parallel past without a problem."

"Since we were not, we ended up here," I concluded.

"That is correct," Milky responded.

"So, Ryton should be here too."

"He is," Milky said. "He is in another part of the buffer. It is like he is here, but he is not here at the same time."

I huffed. "All right then, what happens now?"

"Tempus informed me that you are to choose what happens between you and the other man," Milky stated.

"But it has to agree with both Milky and me since time travel does not only deal with Tempus and her Apostles," Caro added. "You know, the whole space-time continuum, butterfly effect thingy."

"The world already made the mistake of keeping Ryton alive the first time. He has to go, permanently," I spoke.

I'd hate to kill anyone, but what other options do I have that have not been shown to fail?

Caro glanced at Milky. "Well, we've produced a suggestion on how we could help, um, get rid of the Demon King. You know, permanently."

"Wait," I cut her short. "If I am here, does that mean time is frozen on our Earth, Caro?"

She shook her head. "No."

My eyes widened. Arcelia. The sub was sinking!

"Do not worry about the submarine. Lady Death told me, she and Queen Riva got it covered," Caro assured.

"Wait. Riva and the Acolyte of Death are the ones handling a sinking ship? That does not make me feel better," I deadpanned.

"Do not worry," Caro responded. "our fellow Acolyte is the one who planned to sink the sub."

Oh, that's right. Lady Death was the one who got Arcelia and me out of our cells. I knew I didn't see things. And that was why Arcelia knew what was going on.

I rubbed my temples. "Wow, so all of this is part of some plan?"

Milky twirled her finger around a loose strand of hair. "Yes, you can thank your mother for that."

"She planned this?"

Caro tilted her head. "Yes, and no. Archangel had a bit of say in all of this too."

I disregarded what she said. "So, everyone talks about this big Ryton takedown plan, without me?"

I shook my head, pissed. I'm always being left let out when it is essential. I should be used to this by now. Fairly, Tempus did give me the heads up this time around. Nevertheless, I'm tired of being left out. I look around the area. There is nothing here but us. *Yet Ryton is here?* Could he hear us? Could he see us? Well, he can't do anything, it seemed. If he could, he would've done it by now. Hold on.

The gears in my head started to turn. *I got something.*

I focused on the two ladies. "You said you two had a suggestion of what to do with Ryton? Well, I have one of my own. Being here has given me time to think."

Milky focused on me and then Caro.

Caro spoke first. "Okay, Rick, what is it?"

"What if you keep him here and I take care of the Crest and time gate island? He will have to watch the world he wanted to shape so bad, continue here until he dies. Sounds like a good deal?"

I waited for one of them to speak.

"Well, for one," Milky spoke. "this place is a physical barrier of the conception of time and space, so Ryton would be here for eons."

"And secondly, what do we do with Ryton?" Caro asked.

I shrugged. "Once I leave, that is none of my problems."

"Ryton will be under my watchful eye?" Milky asked.

I brushed my hand through my messy hair. "Why not? He will no longer be me or the Earth's problem. Plus, he deserves to suffer from everything he has done and the trouble he has caused on your part."

Caro and Milky shared a glace.

"It is not that bad of an idea. It's better than our idea to just let him die in space," Caro started. "With this, you get something more out of its Ms. Milky."

"The fool will wish he died. If you keep your word and destroy the Crest and the island, I will keep that mutt on a leash," Milky affirmed.

"Sure thing," I said.

Great. How was I supposed to destroy an island?

Milky crossed her four arms. "This is the last time the Space Acolyte or I will clean up the messes of Tempus' servants."

"You mean Apostles," I shot back.

"Rick, please," I glanced at Caro. "Miss Milky is doing a huge favor for you."

Don't you mean us? You are from Earth too.

I decided to let it go and listen to Milky.

"If you do not keep your end of the deal, Ryton will be released back to your world, and you will have to deal with him by yourself," she spoke.

I narrowed my eyes. "If this causes another universe collapse, so be it, right? That does not affect you at all, does it?"

Caro stiffened. "Rick, please."

"It is okay, Caro," I smirked at Milky. "She is bluffing. If Ryton comes back to Earth and is successful in his time travel scheme, rifts in space may begin to form."

Milky's jaw tightened.

"Are you not the ones who have to clean it up? Well, more like watching all your work go to waste," I questioned.

Milky was silent.

Her galaxy eyes stared hollowly at me.

"You are pushing it, Rick," Caro warned.

"It is fine, Caro," Milky stated. "you have a deal, Rodrick."

I looked back at Milky. "Excellent."

I raised my hand for one of her four to shake it. She did so, cautiously.

"You are different from most Tempus Acolytes I've met. Few people would be this gracious or stupid to not up and kill Ryton after what he has done on your planet," Milky inquired.

"I have seen enough death in my hands. And I know if Ryton were to have a death wish, he would want it by my hands. I want to be the first person to not have given him the pleasure of getting his way," I spoke somberly. "And this is how I do that."

Caro smiled at me as Milky smirked. "I still think our plan to finally kill this man would have been better. But this impromptu plan still works. Plus, I get a new plaything out of it."

"Oh, I have one more thing," I started.

She raised an eyebrow. "What is it?"

"Can I talk to him before I go?"

"That is all?" she asked.

"Yes, that is it."

I needed to get some things off my chest before I missed my chance. I didn't know what I was going to say. I knew I had to face him for the second and the final time.

She shrugged. "Very well, Rodrick, you have all the time in the world."

CHAPTER NINETEEN

WAKE UP LOVELY

There were sounds of beeps and the smell of distilled alcohol in the air. Even in the dim light, I could see that most of the room was gray and white. I turned my head to see an expansive window that was shut. I gazed at the table on my right where there was a mountain of stuffed animals, cards, candies, and get-well balloons, crowding it. My body was covered in thin blankets and a light green wrap. *Am I in a hospital?* I tried to sit up when the pain hit me. The door for the room opened.

A woman wearing a dark blue nurse's uniform stepped in. "Good morning, Princess Arcelia. I'm your nurse, Yeema."

I gave a weak smile. "Hello, ma'am. You can call me Arcelia."

She propped the door open, and I heard other nurses and orderlies squeaking shoes echoing through the stagnant room.

Yeema walked over to me with a tray of food. "On a scale of one to ten, how bad is your pain? One being manageable and ten being excruciating."

I held up five fingers.

She placed the food in front of me. "Do you know why you are in the hospital?"

I shook my head. "The last thing I remember..."

The submarine! Rodrick–Oh, no!

"Princess, please relax," she patted my hand. "You're out of harm's way. It is okay. The incident on the...I mean, you got 'sick' two days ago."

"Two days!?"

She started checking my vitals. "Yes, you had to get some minor surgery because of your 'illness.' You have been in and out of consciousness since."

"Where did I get surgery?"

"Your abdomen and lower back."

I gently pushed myself to sit upright. Yeema handed me a glass of water and a few pills. "For after you eat."

"Thank you," I said. "You said I was 'sick'?"

She nodded. "After the A.M.J., you became very ill with food poisoning and were diagnosed with cholestasis."

"Oh."

I put down the glass and medication. "Thank you for letting me know about my 'illness.' I appreciate it."

She chuckled, fluffing my pillows. "You are welcome. Anything else?"

"Could you open the window, too, please?"

She opened the window blinds and shutters.

"Do you want the TV on?"

I shook my head. "No, I am fine."

"You have a few guests waiting for you in the waiting room. Would you like me to tell them they can come in, or would you like to eat something first?"

I shook my head again. "I can eat later. You can tell them to come in."

She smiled. "Certainly, Princess."

She headed to the door. "If you need anything else from me, simply press the button on your bed remote," she pointed to the gray remote sitting on the left side of my hip.

I smiled. "Thank you."

Yeema winked, closing the door on her way out.

Soon I heard a slight knock on the door.

"Come in."

Rodrick, Queen Riva, my mom, and my Auntie Cal were standing in my doorway. Rodrick was holding a giant stuffed griffin with balloons tied around it.

I gave a weak laugh. "Hello, everyone, come in."

"Oh, my baby," my mom engulfed me in a tight hug. I did not have the heart to tell her that she was making my body go numb.

"Hi, Mom, I missed you too," tears started welling in my eyes.

Soon my aunt joined in the hug. Once we let go, I peered at Rodrick and his mother.

"Hello, Queen Riva. Hey, Rodrick."

They both came forward.

"How are you doing, Rodrick?"

He smiled sheepishly. "I'm fine. I'm not the one in a hospital bed."

I laid my head back. "I suppose you're right."

"Of course, I am."

The corners of my lips twitched. "I'm glad you guys came to see me."

"So am I," Rodrick responded.

I felt a pair of eyes on me.

"So, you two were bumping and grinding while you were in hiding?"

I felt my face warm up. "Auntie Cal! *No!*"

Rodrick laughed.

"Honestly, Cal, sizzle down," Mom rolled her eyes.

"Prince Rodrick and Queen Riva wanted to talk to you before they had to leave," Mom said.

I looked at them both.

"We leave tomorrow," Queen Riva spoke. "We could only stay for a few days."

"Well, baby," Aunt Cal started petting my hair. "we will leave you all to talk. When you all are finished, we will come back in."

"Okay, thank you."

Mom and Aunt Cal gave me soft hugs and kisses as they left the room.

Rodrick went and grabbed a chair and placed it at my bedside.

He reached for my hand and gave it a slight squeeze.

Queen Riva cleared her throat. "I want to thank you, Princess Arcelia."

I turned to the queen.

She began to speak. "Thank you for protecting my son. Even though you never needed to do what you did."

She focused on Rodrick. "However, there has been a slight change in his demeanor."

"What do you mean?" I asked.

"What change?" Rodrick questioned.

The sides of her mouth jerked. "Do not worry about it."

Rodrick glanced at his mother. "What is it, Riva?"

She frowned at him. "It's *Māe*. And I will tell you later, in private. I will not be wasting any more of your time, Princess."

"Queen Riva. Thank you for coming."

She lifted her hand. "It is fine."

Her sharp eyes moved toward Rodrick. "The plane takes off at noon."

She started for the door and glanced over her shoulder. "I told Erma to not come back for you if you are late. You will be left behind."

He glanced at me. "I would be fine with that."

I played with the hem of my sheets. "Hush your mouth, Rodrick."

"Get well, Princess. If you ever want to visit the Kingdom of Diar, you are welcome to," Queen Riva concluded.

"I would love to, thank you, Queen."

Riva gave a stiff nod and left the room.

Rodrick groaned. "Arcelia, I am so sorry."

I frowned. "Rodrick, if you came here to apologize, then you and that stuffed griffin can go back to where you came from."

He mustered a smile. "Okay, no apologies. The same goes for you."

I paused. "I should be sorry. I got in the way."

"Arcelia, even I can't change the past. What happened, happened. What matters is that you're okay."

I squeezed his hand. "*We're* okay."

He looked down. "Yeah."

I knit my brow. "Rodrick, after I passed out, what happened? What happened to Ryton?"

"Caro came."

I furrowed my brows. "Caro is...?"

"The Space Acolyte."

"Oh, ok," I said, a bit confused.

"Long story short, Lulu—Lady Death is the one that crashed the submarine."

Yeah, I already knew that.

"She and some others helped arrange that whole sub sinking, and I made a deal with Milky."

"Milky? Like the carton?" I said, perplexed.

He chuckled. "She is the child of Hapesire. I destroyed the Crest and returned the pieces to Taporis. The gateway island had to go to. Lucky for me, that wasn't so hard to do. I will tell you a more detailed story when you get out of the hospital, I promise."

"And Ryton?" I spoke softly.

He let out a breath. "He is gone, not dead, just gone. He can't hurt anyone anymore."

He threaded his fingers through his hair.

I caressed his hand. "What is bothering you?"

He exhaled. "The entire world knows about the submarine, Celia. Other high-ranking Atar officers are making plans to take revenge. The world knows Ryton faked his death."

Rodrick moved his gaze to the floor. "The blindfold has finally been pulled off the eyes of the public, and no one knows whom to trust or believe."

I held his hand. "It'll be okay, Rodrick. You did your part; let the Queen worry about this now. This is not your battle to fight anymore."

He gave me a weak smile. "I hope so. I have to attend a conference when we go back to Diar."

There was a soft knock on the door.

"Prince Rodrick, you two have been in there for a while. Everything okay?" My mom questioned.

He sighed. "Guess I should be leaving."

He got up slowly. "I left my number in one of the cards."

"Cards? Like more than one?"

Rodrick shrugged. "I couldn't decide which one was best for you."

I hold back a smile. "You idiot."

He rolled his eyes. "When you find it, call me, okay?"

I grinned widely. "I will."

He reached and pushed my hair from my face.

"You want to kiss my forehead?" I joked.

"I rather kiss something else."

I gazed at his eyes; I could not tell if he was joking or serious.

He planted a kiss on my head. He smelled good, as usual, but the scent was homier.

I frowned when he moved moves away.

He laughed at my expression. "Why are you pouting?"

"That is not my lips," I responded. "I risk my life for you, and all I get is a kiss on the forehead?"

He chuckled. "I saved your life afterward."

I sucked air through my teeth. "Did you?"

He ran his empty hand through his hair. "You are going to be a handful."

I smacked my lips. "What does that mean?"

There was another knock on the door. "You two done kissing yet!?" Aunt Cal asks.

He laughed.

"No, not yet!" Rodrick responded.

"If I had the strength to hit you, I would," I whispered.

He chuckled again as he leaned down—

"Arcelia, I know you are not smacking lips with that boy!"

I groaned at my mom's behavior; Rodrick laughed.

He kissed me on the forehead again and once on the lips. "Yes, we are Queen Fayola!"

"RODRICK!" My mom yelled.

"Don't worry," he peered down at me. "I'm done."

He leaned toward my ear, whispering. "*For now.*"

He pulled away with a wink.

I tried my best to hide my delight. "Bye, Rodrick."

He kissed my hand. "Until next time, *minha bela princesa.*"

CHAPTER TWENTY

As I switched through the dials of the radio, I tried to calm my thoughts. Finally, I reached a news station and turned the volume dial-up.

"…This is Jeanna Kyles reporting from the scene unfolding here at Crilima's largest airport, Tamalan International. Louis, I must tell you, it is a horrific scene down here. The police and medical teams, as you can hear behind me, are working frantically within and outside of the airport. From the information we have now, there are about 48 people who are concluded to be dead…."

I scoffed.

Only 48 people? How laughable.

"…This is the highest number of deaths in an incident like this that Crilima has ever seen. The suspect's whereabouts are unknown. Although forces are saying that this may have been a suicide bombing or terrorist attack, possibly by the Atar..."

I took a long sip from my glass of *white* wine.

"...Investigators are working on the meaning of the symbol left behind after the bombing…."

I furrowed my eyebrows. "What symbol?"

"...A symbol which some sources believe is in honor of the Demon King..."

I smiled madly.

"Your life will not go in vain, my King."

I gazed at my picture of His Majesty. I touched the surface, guiding my claws down it.

"Long live the King. You will rise."

END

SNEAK PEEK

Here's a sneak peek inside the next book in *The Gods' Scion* series: *Descendants of Time and Death.*

I was sitting on something soft and grimy. It was sinking under me a bit, which startled me. Sand, but it was gray. I was alone in a vast, dark, and quiet wasteland. The sun was shining hard and bright.

"Lulonah." An eerie child voice spoke.

I looked around. "Yes?"

There was no one there. I got up, trying to get a better look at where I was. The only landmarks were more miles of barren and empty grey sand.

"He can save us…."

I turned around quickly, again, no one. "Who is there?"

I looked around anxiously.

It was a child before now; it sounded like an old man.

The winds picked up softly. My dark, black hair whipped in my face.

"You will try, but you cannot…."

My eyes widened; I knew that voice. I turned around.

"Nikolai—"

My eyes moved around everywhere, trying to see any glimpse of my husband.

As I took a step, a loud crunch came from under my foot.

I looked down; it was the decaying head of a young child. Their hair had fallen out along with most of their teeth. Bugs and maggots crawled all over their rotting flesh.

Screaming, I quickly stepped back, falling. I felt sick to my stomach. I covered my mouth, forcing myself not to vomit.

I looked up at the sky. It was dark grey and blue.

The winds blew stronger. I looked ahead.

The empty wasteland now had a hill in the center of it, piled high with dead bodies.

Men, women, and children, young and old. Bloody and soulless eyes bored into my eyes.

"No," I struggled to my feet. "No—"

Multiple hands grabbed me. I looked at the decaying bodies surrounding me, trying to weigh me down.

"You cannot save us…he can save us…time is not in your favor…."

Another group of hands grabbed my left arm and successfully pulled me down into a growing pit.

"Please, I'm sorry, I want to—"

A golden light shone above the pit.

A man walked into my vision. He had shoulder-length red hair, creamy skin, and deep blue eyes.

"Rodrick!"

He reached his hand out. "I can save those who he cannot reach in time."

Trying to reach for his hand as I sank in deeper and deeper.

"Rodrick!"

…To Be Continued…

APPENDIX

MAP OF EARTH

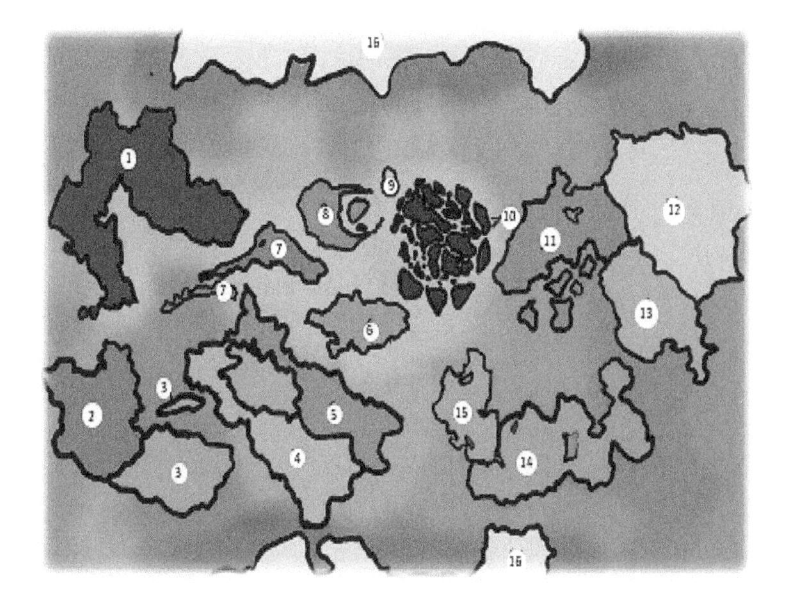

Number	Country
1	Diar
2	Qirar
3	Sevodric
4	Kedaele
5	Sevoelle
6	Chaparrals
7	Boscages of Waeven
8	Cadaliri
9	Crilima
10	Amarem
11	The Sanguine Palisades
12	Siesa Arid
13	Şahvar
14	Lomar
15	Lands of Xau
16	Artica

THE COUNTRIES OF THE WORLD

Country's Name	*Name Articulation*	*Country Leader(s)*	*Official Language(s)*
Amarem	*aa-ma-rim*	Czar Alyen and Czarina Nalani	*Porta*
Boscages of Waeven	*boss-cages of wave-in*	Queen Mouna Keita	*Cree*
Ca Cadaliri	*ca-da-lee-ear-ee*	King Dalite	*Cree*
Chaparrals	*shh-a-pa-rr-als*	General Maharani Ariella-Zalea	*Anglish*
Crilima	*k-rr-l-im-ma*	President Vilas and First Lady Malaia	*Sevo*
Diar	*die-air*	Queen Riva	*Porta*
Kedaele	*key-da-lay*	King Muriell and Queen Naline	*Linga and Anglish*
Lands of Xau	*lands of z-ah-zoo*	Queen Le Mai of the Ruling Lands of Xau	*Xain*
Lomar	*low-ma-rr*	Empress Jade Chartreuse of the High Court	*Loma*
Qirar	*key-are ('q' is pronounced as a 'k')*	Sister Queens Fayola and Calandra	*Linga and Anglish*
Şahvar	*sa-var*	President Sol	*None*

The Sanguine Palisades	*san-gee-in pal-iss-aid-iss*	King Hazmin and Queen Misrah	*Arian*
Sevodric	*see-no-dr-ick (the 'v' and pronounced as a 'n')*	King Brandeles and Lady Lalita	*Sevo*
Sevoelle	*see-no-elle (the 'v' and pronounced as an 'n')*	Count Fabian and Countess Mistral	*Sevo*
Siesa Arid	*sea-ss-ah air-id*	Sultana Ephedra–Rosanna	*Arian*

Country	Continent	Topography
Amarem	Coscos	Archipelago
Boscages of Waeven	Coscos	Rainforest
Cadaliri	Coscos	Volcanic beach
Chaparrals	Coscos	Temperate Rainforest
Crilima	Coscos	Island
Diar	Eruais	Taiga
Kedaele	Otia	Mountainous plains
Lands of Xau	Juade	Rolling hills
Lomar	Juade	Humid plains
Qirar	Otia	Lowlands
Şahvar	Nazcan	Valley lands
The Sanguine Palisades	Nazcan	Volcanic desert
Sevodric	Otia	Deciduous forest
Sevoelle	Otia	Grasslands
Siesa Arid	Nazcan	Sandy deserts

THE EMBLEM OF TEMPUS

ABOUT THE AUTHOR

Winnifred or Winnie, as most know her by, is an artist, writer, and author of her debut novel, *The Gods' Scion: Child of Tempus*. As a military child, Winnie has traveled extensively around the US East Coast and Germany, learning about the history, lore, and culture of each region. Winnie has spent the last two years writing and expanding the world of *The Gods' Scion* trilogy series. Winnie has a lifelong love of literature and art. As a new writer, she wants to create a beautiful fantasy world and with compelling and intriguing characters. Winnie lives in South Carolina and is an undergraduate at the College of Charleston. She loves to spread positivity and joy to those around her and look at the world through a glittery pink lens.

You can follow Winnie on her book journeys through her blog:
https://winsbooks.blog

Made in the USA
Middletown, DE
19 January 2024